W9-BAU-899

FRONTIER JUSTICE

Book Three: Virginia

FRONTIER JUSTICE

Book Three: Virginia

•

DON HEPLER

AVALON BOOKS
THOMAS BOUREGY AND COMPANY, INC.
401 LAFAYETTE STREET
NEW YORK, NEW YORK 10003

Library of Congress Catalog Card Number: 95-96088
ISBN 0-8034-9160-3

PRINTED IN THE UNITED STATES OF AMERICA
ON ACID-FREE PAPER
BY HADDON CRAFTSMEN, SCRANTON, PENNSYLVANIA

FRONTIER JUSTICE

Book Three: Virginia

Chapter One

Walter Donnahue carefully lined up the small golden bead at the end of the rifle barrel with the notch close to his eye until they rested in the center of the man's chest. He had done the same thing many, many times, mostly with buffalo. Shooting men didn't really seem a whole lot different except it was kind of exciting later to go down and see what they had owned up until the time he killed them. It was sort of like a treasure hunt.

The man driving the wagon had no idea his life was about to end, and that was just the way Walter liked it. The fewer risks he took, the more likely he was to live to a ripe old age.

The moment of killing—no, the moment just *before* killing—always hung over him. He was very aware that with a slight effort of his trigger finger something important was about to happen, something that could never be undone. It was a feeling of power, especially when his sights were lined up on a man. Important as that man's life was to that man, Walter could snatch it away with such a little amount of effort that it still seemed incredible to him.

The man stretched and began a yawn, and somehow Walter found it amusing to shoot him in mid-yawn. He tightened his finger slightly and the .50-caliber Sharps slammed back in his shoulder and boomed loudly. The man died with his mouth wide open, the heavy slug slamming him backward into the interior of his wagon. The horses stopped obediently at the tug on their reins by the already dead hand, and for a moment there was silence. Then the screaming began.

It was the screaming of a young woman, and it was coming from inside the wagon. Walter was amazed. He had done this four times before, and never had any of the men had anybody with them. Obviously this man was different, and it certainly complicated things a bunch. He stayed prone on the ground and thought it over.

He could leave, in which case nobody could ever know what he had done. Of course that would mean that all the treasures in that wagon would escape him. He could stay where he was and wait for the girl to come out and kill her too, only Walter wasn't crazy about the idea of shooting a girl. Killing boys was okay, but there was something almost sacred about females as far as he was concerned. Besides, the other men in the West did not take kindly to killers of women. It was a dilemma sure enough.

He rolled on his back and stared at the sky as he listened to the girl scream and cry. The sky was blue with puffy white clouds hanging in the west. A grasshopper buzzed by; he watched it land on a piece of grass just out of reach. The screaming slowly subsided into loud crying.

The idea came to him all at once, like a bolt of lightning. He examined it from every angle, and the more he looked at it the better it seemed. Might be that wagon held a treasure he hadn't ever counted on or expected. The audacity of the idea appealed to his sense of humor, and he smiled at the grasshopper before rolling over and walking back to his horse.

Katie Withrow had been lying on the bed resting when her father was killed and fell back into the wagon to land right on top of her. At first it had been so confusing when it happened—Father just hurtling back on top of her with no reason. It was only later that she could remember hearing the distant bang of a rifle.

He had fallen on top of her and she struggled under him until she could get out from under. It was then that she felt his slippery blood on her dress and her hands. She looked closer at Father, and saw the raw meat that had once been his back. This was too much for a sixteen-year-old girl to understand or accept. It was then that she started to scream.

Already it seemed so long ago, so much like a dream.

She finished buttoning her blue dress, then took the bloody green one that had been her favorite and tossed it out the back of the moving wagon. She could no longer see the bloody quilt she had tossed out earlier.

She dug out her hairbrush that had once been her mother's and pulled it through her hair absently a few times, then tucked it back and crawled out the front of the wagon to sit next to the man who had come along and doubtless saved her life. He looked over at her.

"You look a sight better," he said. Walter had enjoyed looking back through the crack in the canvas and watching the girl change clothes in the moving wagon. Women were special people and being around them could make a man feel good all over. Young women were even better, and he had never in his wildest dreams ever imagined he would get a chance to watch what he had just watched. It was all he could do not to crawl back there with her, only he figured that maybe he could come out of this even better if he played his cards close to his vest.

"I feel better," she said. She looked up at him impassively. His expression showed a concern for her that she somehow found comforting. It was so hard to accept that Father was gone and the Lord had seen fit to replace him for the moment with this man.

He had come riding up fast; then he pulled her father's body out and started driving the wagon fast.

"Don't know why they haven't come down on you yet," he said. "I been running from them myownself for a good part of the day."

"Running from who?" she asked, and could still remember the chill up her back when he said the hated word.

"Indians," he said, and that was almost enough. She still wanted to go back for Father so she could bury him good and proper.

"No," said the man. "That's probably what they want us to do so they can catch us out of the wagon. He ain't in that body anymore, nohow. He's with the Lord lookin' down on us, and likely he'd want us to git on out o' here right prompt."

That had seemed to make pretty good sense to her, especially when she remembered the whispered stories among the giggling girls about what the Indians would do with a girl if they caught her.

"Are they going to come after us?" she asked. He appeared to think about it.

"I doubt it," he said. "They know I am a good shot and likely will not want to tangle with me again as long as we keep moving. They will likely just lick their wounds and settle for having killed that man driving the wagon."

"That was my father," she said. His eyes saddened.

"I am truly sorry, miss," he said. He drove in silence for a minute, then said, "Name's Walter. Walter Donnahue."

"Hello, Walter," Katie said politely. "I am Katie Withrow." He nodded but said nothing. She looked out over the prairie that no longer looked as lovely as it had that very morning.

"Thank you," she said. "Thank you for coming when I screamed, and thank you for saving my life." He shrugged.

"Any man would'a done it," he said. "I just happened to be the only one around."

"Thank you anyway, Mr. Donnahue."

"Walter," he said. "You can call me Walter."

"Thank you, Walter."

"You are surely welcome, miss," he said. Katie sighed and relaxed as much as she could on a moving wagon seat. It looked like the Lord had seen her through. Things would be all right. Thank God for Walter.

"Thank God for you, Walter," she said. He looked down at her strangely for a moment, then smiled like he knew something she didn't.

"Yeah, miss," he said. "You sure are lucky I came along."

* * *

Wiley had picked up the wagon tracks shortly after sunup. He couldn't really say why he had turned and followed them except maybe it was because they were the only tracks he had seen for two days. They looked to be about two days old, and it was unusual to find a wagon headed north instead of west, so he swung his horse around and followed along. North appeared to be just as good a direction as any, since the villain's tracks had faded out after the rain two days ago. Maybe the folks in the wagon could tell him something about the man he was hunting.

He had been following the trail for about two hours before he discovered that the wagon contained two people, not just one. There were signs of a small-footed person who walked alongside the wagon a piece before he—or more likely she—got back in to ride once more. Man driving the wagon must've had his wife along, or maybe his daughter. Somehow Wiley knew it was a man driving the wagon, mostly because it was inconceivable that two women would be out here all alone.

It was almost sundown when he came on the body; he reined in and looked around carefully. The man had obviously been dead the better part of the day, so it was unlikely that the perpetrator of this evil action was still in the vicinity, but it never hurt to be real careful when killing was concerned.

Before getting down to examine the body, he began riding in ever larger circles, trying to find any signs of the killer before the sun got too low in the sky. There was a small bluff about a hundred and fifty yards away, and it was here that he found the empty shell. He swung down and picked it up.

It was from a .50-caliber, a buffalo gun most likely. The firing pin hit a little off center, and it had a slight bulge that left its mirror image in the cap. If he found another shell from the same gun he could tell easy enough. He tucked the shell case in his saddlebag and studied the spot where the killer had lain in wait.

He could still see where the man had been and where he had rolled over, likely looking at the sky while waiting for the wagon to come along. There was no doubt that the dead man had been driving the wagon, it was the only way the thing could have figured out. The killer had planned it out, lying here and waiting until the wagon showed up, then up and shooting the driver from ambush.

He mounted and followed the killer's tracks as he had gone to where his horse had been waiting. The boots had three hobnails on the bottom, and would also be easy to spot. His horse had been there for a considerable length of time too, maybe three or four hours, from all the cropped grass and piles of manure. Wiley shook his head slightly. It took a certain kind of man to just lay in wait for that long to kill someone. Maybe there was real hatred between them, or maybe it was just simple robbery by a man to whom life held no value. Or maybe—and here he bit his lip slightly—it had something to do with the woman.

He followed the killer's tracks as he rode around the site of the murder at almost a mile distant, then came right up to the wagon at a run and stopped hard. He had dismounted, likely tossed the body from the wagon, and driven off at a pretty good rate of speed. There was no sign of the woman at all.

He dismounted and went over to examine the body. The man had been shot dead-center in the chest and the big slug had removed a pretty good-size chunk of his back when it had blasted through his body. Not a bad shot considering the range. The victim hadn't done a whole lot of bleeding on the grass, so he was obviously shot and killed in the wagon and dumped after he was dead.

Wiley studied the bloody handprints on the man's shirt. The woman had held him most likely, held him and then pushed him away, least that was the story the prints told. Small hands. Small woman, likely. Maybe no more than a girl.

The man's pockets were empty, one of them even turned inside out. Whatever he'd had on him was taken.

Wiley took the small shovel off his packhorse and began to dig. No matter who the man was, he deserved a decent burial. Besides, it was going to be dark soon, and there was no way he could possibly catch up with them today. He felt really bad about the unknown woman or girl, but likely whatever was going to happen to her had already happened. Even if it hadn't there was nothing he could do for her until he caught up with them. If they stayed in the wagon, that would likely be tomorrow.

Nope. All he could do was bury the poor man and try not to think about what might be going on in that wagon. He patted the earth into a mound that would disappear with the first rain.

"There you are, mister," he said to the grave. "For whatever it is worth I give you my word I will track him down and he will answer to the law for doin' you in like that." He turned to make camp, then turned back. "I'll make him pay for whatever he has done to your woman too," he promised.

He swung into the saddle and booted his horse into motion, packhorse behind. He had come across a pretty good arroyo just a ways ahead when he had been circling the body earlier. He would camp there.

The sun glowed red on the western horizon and the grave was soon left in the absolute silence of dusk just before the prairie comes alive with night creatures. The wind rustled some of the long grass softly and the grave smelled of fresh-dug earth. A few seeds from the nearby grass drifted on the wind and settled on the mounded soil.

Walter pulled the team to a halt and crawled down, stretching noisily. The setting sun glared down balefully, casting everything with a tint of red.

He helped Katie down, feeling her warmth and softness through her gingham dress, holding onto her just a second longer than necessary. It was as if he was tormenting himself with her. As if he enjoyed having her there. At his mercy. If he wanted.

"Thank you, Walter," she said, and rested her hand on his arm for a moment. It was like fire where she touched him.

He cleared a fire circle, took some of the deadwood she had gathered, and lit a cooking fire. He put the grate across the flames and went to see to the horses, confident that Katie would start cooking the two rabbits he had shot earlier.

He picketed the horses and brushed them down carefully. After all, they were his now, even if Katie didn't know it yet. By the time he was finished, the sun was half gone and he could smell food cooking on the breeze. He went over to lean on the wagon and watch the girl at work. She smiled up at him and brought him a cup of fresh coffee.

"Thank you," he heard himself say, and she smiled brightly and went back to her work. Walter sipped at the coffee and watched her at the fire.

"If you would get the table down," she said,

"we can eat in a more civilized fashion. No need to squat on the ground like savages."

He took the small table from the wagon and put two straight-backed chairs at either end, then picked up his cup and resumed leaning.

The pots were steaming wondrous smells into the still evening air, and she finally called him to supper just as his cup was empty.

He sat at the table, and it felt almighty strange out in the middle of the prairie like that. She brought him a plate piled high with pieces of rabbit cooked crisp and brown, with fried potatoes, sourdough rolls, and more coffee. It was a meal fit for a man, and he dug in with gusto. She sat down opposite him and also began to eat.

"This is great," he said through a mouthful. She smiled across at him.

"I am glad you like it, Walter," she said.

He ate one full plate and did not complain when she took the empty plate and filled it once more. He forced the last bite down just as she set an open can of peaches in front of him.

"Here, Walter," she said. "Tonight we have peaches to celebrate your coming along to save my life." He mumbled something about her being welcome, and speared a golden peach from the can. Full as he was, the fruit was delicious and sweet, and in no time he had eaten almost all of them.

Walter finally set down his fork, picked up his cup of coffee, and leaned back dangerously in the chair.

"Oh, lord," he said. "I am stuffed clean to the top. Cannot fit in another bite anywhere." She laughed like a delighted schoolgirl.

"Good," she said. "I knew I could fill you up and do it right too."

"Food was great, Katie," he admitted. He sipped at his coffee and watched her finish eating. She picked up her food daintily, eating clean and neat, not at all the way he had shoveled it down. Girls certainly were interesting critters to watch, he thought.

"You do not drink coffee?" he asked, surprised some.

"No," she said and smiled like a little girl. She gave a shrug. "I just never like the taste is all." She acted like it was a shameful secret, and he laughed, which was what she had wanted all along.

A full day and a full belly acted fast on a man, and he was yawning hard and long before she was half done cleaning the dishes. He watched her working around the camp and contemplated on going to her and taking her in his arms, but the weariness was overpowering. She would be there when he woke up, and his bedroll was calling to him loud and long. He rose and stretched, listening to his tendons crack.

"I am fixin' to turn in, Katie," he said to her.

"Ohhh," she said. She sounded a little disappointed. "I was hoping we could talk some. You know, maybe find out a little about each other."

"I'd like that," he responded. "I surely would, but it has been a long day and tomorrow will be another chance."

"I'm sorry," she said. "I should have thought about you first. You go ahead and turn in. I just want to finish up the dishes and then I'll go to bed too."

"'Night," he said, and headed for his bedroll. He couldn't remember when he had been so tired. Rough day what with the killin' and playactin' and all. He grinned to himself. Man had to really be tired to leave such a pretty little girl go wanting like that.

He took off his boots, rolled into his blankets, and was asleep in minutes. Last thing he heard was the girl humming to herself as she finished washing the dishes. Sounded real natural and pleasant somehow.

Katie finished the last of the dishes, then sat on the chair and stared into the dying fire. She glanced over at Walter sound asleep under the wagon and let her emotions drain out of her. Father was dead. Back there somewhere. Unburied. Dead. Gone forever.

She felt her eyes brim over with tears, then the hot trail as the wetness of her pain slid down each cheek. She would never hear his laugh, never feel his touch, never see his face again. Not as long as she lived. Never again would he teach her or be able to help her. First Mother. Then Father. It wasn't fair. Life was so hard and she was so young.

For five minutes she cried, then wiped her face and sighed. Life was hard all right. But it kept on, relentless and unyielding. And she had to keep on too. Father was gone and so was Mother, but she had their memories. She could bring them forth at will, talk to them in her mind. In a way they would be with her always.

She got to her feet and walked to the wagon. She could hear Walter snoring gently underneath the wagon, and wondered if he was dreaming. She knelt down and looked at the sleeping man for a long minute, studying what little of his face she could see in the dark. After a minute or two, she smiled at his sleeping form, then stood up and crawled inside the wagon. She let down her hair in the dark, doing the familiar act by feel, then adjusted the blankets into her bed. She eased down on her back, thinking about her father, eyes wide open in the dark.

Finally, when the cool began to seep into her, she pulled a blanket up to her chin and closed her eyes. Walter snored easily under the floor.

Life was hard and she was so young.

It took her a long, long time to get to sleep.

Walter woke to find the morning sky full of leaden gray clouds that seemed to match his mood. He lay there under the wagon for a few minutes, looking at the dull day. His head hurt; it felt sort of thick. Maybe he was coming down with something.

He could hear the girl humming as she bustled around the fire, and he could smell the coffee. She was one tough girl, he had to admit, losing her father like that, yet keeping on keeping on. It was enough to make a man proud of her. In a way, he was ashamed of doing her father like he had done. 'Course, he would have never met her otherwise. It seemed as though God had a plan for everything—even murderers.

He wriggled out of the bedroll and sat up to pull on his boots. A wave of dizziness washed through him, and he had to put out his hand to steady himself on the wagon. Yup. He was coming down with something, sure enough. He fought back the queasy feeling, pulled on his boots, and got to his feet. Katie saw him and smiled brightly.

"Morning, Walter," she said.

"Morning," he said right back.

"Looks like it might rain later today, huh?" She was so cheerful it almost annoyed him. It was probably just on account of his coming sickness though, so he fought back the twinge of anger and forced a smile. ''Might,'' he said.

''Breakfast be ready in a minute,'' said Little Miss Sunshine.

''Fine,'' he said, and headed out away from the wagon. Suddenly the idea of a trip to the backhouse had a powerful lot of draw. The next fifteen minutes were not some of the most pleasant in his re-collection. When he came back, he was pale and trembling, cold sweat beaded on his face. Katie looked at him in sudden concern.

''You all right?'' she asked. ''You were gone so long, and to tell the truth, you don't look so good.'' Walter sank gratefully onto one of the chairs.

''Tell you true,'' he said, ''I am a little under the weather this morning. Maybe something I ate.''

''I don't think so,'' she came back. ''I ate the same food as you, and I feel fine.''

''So you did,'' he admitted. He sighed, and another wave of dizziness swept through him. ''Maybe I just need to eat some and I'll be all right.''

''Breakfast is coming up, sir,'' she said and beamed a big grin at him. Walter didn't grin back, and after a moment of waiting, she shrugged and turned back to her cooking. In a minute she set a cup of coffee in front of him. Walter forced himself to raise the cup to his lips and sip.

Yup. He was sick sure enough. Only yesterday the idea of a woman-made cup of coffee first thing in the morning would have been close to his idea of heaven. Today, he could barely force down more than a sip or two. Katie set a plate of duck eggs and sourdough toast in front of him.

''Here,'' she said. ''Eat up. Maybe it'll help you fight off whatever's wrong.''

That made pretty good sense to Walter, so he took up his fork and began to eat. The first bite almost congealed in his mouth, but he forced himself to eat the eggs and bread, forced down every bite. He didn't want to get sick now. He had this girl with him, and he had plans for her.

He leaned back in his chair and watched her eat opposite him. Maybe she was right about the food. He did feel a little bit better. He took up his cup.

"Wait!" she said, mouth full. "I'll get you some hot coffee." He nodded and dumped the cold stuff into the grass. His head still hurt, but his stomach felt a little better. He was going to have to go out into the grass again shortly, though. She poured the steaming hot liquid into his cup.

"Thanks," he said, and she waved it off. She returned to her eating while he sipped at the brew.

She sure was a good-looker, with a straight nose and wide mouth. Her dress bulged just where it should, and she moved with the easy grace of youth. She'd have to call herself a woman before he was through with her, and the thought brought a small smile to his lips. His bowels rumbled furiously and he rose to his feet hastily.

"Back in a minute," he said, and headed away from the wagon once more. At least if he was going to get sick, he'd have her to take care of him. She'd probably take good care of him too, on account of she figured she owed him her life. The thought made him smile as he hurried into the tall grass.

Chapter Two

Midmorning found Wiley back on the trail of the wagon, riding steadily between the easily followed wheel tracks. It was a beautiful day, sky deep blue and not too hot. Bees were buzzing around and all was right with the world. Only thing was, Wiley was kind of lonesome. He was a little embarrassed to admit it even to himself, but he missed the company of his friend and former partner, Nestor. Nestor had just taken a sheriff job back in Fleet on account of marrying that Rebecca girl. Now the great outdoors just seemed a little empty without him.

He rode up on the spot where the wagon had stopped for the night and wasted only a little time examining the area.

The horses, two of them, had eaten the grass down in an enclosed area, so they had probably made a rope corral for the night. The small cooking fire had been carefully extinguished and it looked like the man had slept under the wagon—alone. Wiley pondered on that, but it could mean almost anything.

Maybe the woman was dead in the wagon, or

maybe the killer had a trace of decency in him. Or maybe she was just an awful ugly woman. Wiley took position between the wheel marks and rode on after them. He figured he was maybe three or four hours behind now.

Come noon, he took some jerky and chewed while he rode. The salt tasted good in his mouth. He took his canteen, pulled the cork, and drank four swallows, no more. No idea how long that water would have to last him, although it was likely there was plenty all around. Conserving water was just a good habit to get into out in the wilderness.

He took the cork, stuck it in, and popped it home with his fist.

The next thing he knew, he was flat on his back looking into the blazing sun with no idea how he got there. He must've been unconscious for a second. The sun was brilliant in his eyes, and he squinted against its power. He had no feeling at all in the left side of his shoulder or his left arm. When he looked down and saw the stain on the left side of his chest, it took him a long moment before he realized the stain was blood—his blood—and he had been shot. He had never heard the sound at all.

He remembered what that murdered man had looked like yesterday with the big piece of his back blown out, and imagined he must look pretty much the same way. He was kind of surprised that it didn't hurt like he had always figured it would. Nope. Just sort of a general numbness on the left side. He could easily feel the warm wetness of his own blood on his chest and stomach, and that was a little uncomfortable. Everything began to fade and waver, and he figured he was about to black out, probably forever.

Somehow he pulled his bandanna from around his neck, reached around behind him with his right hand, and pushed the crumpled cloth against the raw meat back there, then laid back on the ground, pressing it tight against the awful wound. It was kind of pointless really, but something inside wouldn't let him just give up and die without doing everything he could to stay alive.

Whoever shot him, that killer most likely would come to be certain he was dead, so Wiley pulled his pistol and held it in his right hand on the ground. Maybe he could stay conscious long enough to get a little back from the villain who had shot him.

He lay there looking up at the sun and listening to the bees and bugs in the prairie. He could hear every beat of his heart. The sun didn't seem near so bright anymore and it got quieter and quieter, then he realized he couldn't feel the gun in his hand anymore. In fact, he couldn't feel anything. And then there was nothing.

It was the first time Katie had been alone since yesterday, the first time alone since her father had been killed, and Katie caught her breath at the overpowering sense of emptiness that suddenly overcame her. Walter had taken his horse on their backtrail to "see if them Indians are still back there," and to watch him ride away like that was unpleasant to say the least. It was amazing how much she had come to depend on this man since he had showed up only yesterday.

She kept the walking horses headed north like he had said, constantly looking back to see the first sign of his return. The hours bled away slowly, and it was afternoon before she saw his form riding up her backtrail. At first she wasn't certain it was him, then she recognized his shape in the saddle. The awful aloneness, the fear he would not return, vanished. He rode up alongside.

"Any Indians?" she asked.

"Nope," came the laconic reply. Even though he looked a little pale and sickly under his tan, Katie wished he would tie his horse on the back and ride up beside her. In a few minutes, that's just what he did, and then she could feel his shoulder next to her every time the wagon jolted on a bump. He took the reins from her, brushing her hands as he did so.

"I expected you to have some fresh meat with you," she said finally. He looked over at her.

"Oh yeah?" he asked. "How come?"

"I thought I heard a shot before," she said. He nodded.

"I took a shot at a deer," he explained. "Too far away and I missed."

"Too bad. Fresh meat would have been nice."

"Maybe for you. I ain't real hungry anyway," he admitted. The silence stretched out, but it was a comfortable silence. Finally Katie broke it.

"I'm glad you're back," she said, eyes cast down. In spite of his pounding head and twitchy innards Walter grinned at her.

"It's nice to see you again too," he said.

Virginia McGilliam was twenty-three years old and bald. Not just a little bit bald either, but bald all over. Most people have little hairs on their arms, some fuzz on their cheeks, but not Virginia. She had no eyebrows, no eyelashes, not a single hair anywhere.

To look at her a body wouldn't notice her affliction because she always wore man's clothes, with a bandanna tied around her shiny head and usually covered with a man's hat. The clothes had been her father's and were large for her, the vest hanging almost to her knees, the trousers bunched up at her waist where she used one of Dad's belts with an extra hole punched in it to hold them up. Likely as not, the long end of the belt would slip from the loop and dangle down between her legs.

She always wore boots with the trousers tucked in the top, and because she was of diminutive nature, the boot tops came halfway up her lower legs. She would wear one of Dad's cloth coats over this outfit, the garment almost reaching her knees. Mostly she would leave the coat unbuttoned unless it was cold outside.

On the whole she presented a figure that would definitely attract a lot of attention in any populated area. Which wasn't a problem because she didn't live in any populated area. She didn't even live close to one.

Mom and Dad had died of the croup within two days of each other and suddenly Virginia was alone in the wagon that had carried the three of them for so long. She had buried them side by side, unhitched the team and settled down right there in spite of the attempts of the others to keep her with the wagon train. Her folks had company where they lay, for the croup had taken quite a toll at this particular location. Altogether there were eight wooden crosses out there.

Virginia had watched the train until it was gone over the horizon, then set to working making a home. She still had hair at that time, although it was less than a week when she first noticed a silver dollar-size area on her head that was devoid of hair.

In less than a month, she was completely bald. All over.

It was like further punishment from above, maybe because she had not saved her folks from coughing themselves to death, and even though it was pretty strange, she was working so hard trying to stay alive that she had managed to live with the condition without too much shame. Still and all, it was then that she took to wearing a bandanna all the time.

When she looked in the looking glass that had been her mother's, she thought she looked sort of like a gypsy, what with the colorful cloth on her head, but her appearance didn't bother her too much because she never saw any other person.

Staying alive was not the easiest thing to do, either.

She had parked the wagon in the grove of trees by the curve in the creek and made a lean-to, then put in a small crop with some of the most backbreaking work she had ever done. The prairie sod was laced with countless tiny roots and almost impossible to cut through, so she used an ax. Then she peeled back the layers of sod, using the ax and a shovel to cut it loose from the dirt below. She took the sod and began to lay out the shape of a small soddy, one room only, then returned and started removing the next piece.

Day after endless day, making maybe twenty feet by three feet of cleared land in a day, she worked on. Life was hard and she lived on supplies from the wagon and meat from animals that she shot herself as she planted her first crop and hoped it was not too late in the season to reap a harvest. She was sixteen at the time.

Now, seven years later, she was lean and hard as

the land itself. Her hands were tough and callused like a man's hands, and she had a small two-room cabin made of wood she cut into boards by herself. The fireplace was made of fieldstone, and it drew well and kept the cabin warm in the winter.

She had a good ten acres of cleared land that she worked, harvesting meager crops of corn and beans and potatoes. It was enough to live on and even put some away for the winter.

Last year she had put a plank floor down, and the windows all had curtains made of some of the gay-colored cloth Mom had packed to take along. She had made the curtains last year because there was nothing to do in the winter except sew anyway.

Occasionally she would hitch the team and drive the wagon thirty miles to town. Folks there considered her a little strange because of all the clothes she wore, but Virginia paid them no mind. She would sell what little things she had found on the prairie that had been left behind by folks with overloaded wagons. Sometimes she would have extra crops to sell, like potatoes or beans. She would then buy what she needed and leave, glad to be gone from the sight of other people, for her hair had never come back.

It was on just such a trip, headed back for the solitude and safety of her secluded home, that she came across the man on the prairie. She reined in and looked down at the man lying faceup in the grass. She studied him for a few moments, then began to speak. She spoke very little in town, but it was one of the things she did a lot when she was alone.

''Just my luck you aren't dead, I bet,'' she said. The man didn't move; his eyes were closed. She could see the spot of red on his chest and she looked around uneasily.

"Somebody saw fit to put a bullet into you, didn't they?" She felt the big pistol on her belt, hoping that whoever shot this man was long gone, then made up her mind and crawled down from the wagon. She knelt by the prone figure, keeping her hand close to her gun and examined him.

"Well, you aren't dead," she said, "but mighty near." It was as if she could feel eyes on her from somewhere, but she felt like that a lot, especially when some of her baldness was showing, so she ignored the feeling.

"I suppose you think I am going to take you in and tend to you," she said. "I could, you know, but I am not sure I could save you anyhow. An awful lot of your blood has leaked out. Probably a lot of pretty flowers are going to grow up here next spring." She saw where his horses had grazed and followed the trail to a small hollow where two horses were grazing contentedly. She walked up to them and caught up the reins.

"Come with me, horses," she said. "No sense in letting you go to waste out here." She led the horses to the wagon and tied them on the back. One of them was a packhorse and likely had some good stuff. She walked over to the man again and looked down on him.

"You dead yet?" she asked. His chest still rose and fell as he took shallow breaths.

"Not yet, huh?" she said. She stood there looking down on him, uncertain what to do, then she saw the pistol under his hand. Virginia knelt down and moved his hand. His skin felt warm and alive and gave her a funny feeling when she touched it. She took the pistol and put it back in the man's holster. She began to unfasten the gunbelt—likely he wouldn't need it anymore—when his hand suddenly grabbed her wrist and she bleated in fear. His eyes were open and he was looking her dead in the eye. His face was pale and beaded with sweat.

"You an angel?" he asked weakly.

"Not even close, mister," she said. She worked her wrist loose. He didn't seem to have a lot of strength left.

"Wiley," he said softly. "Name is Wiley Board." His eyes closed and for a moment she thought he was out cold again, but they flicked open once more.

"You the one who shot me?" he wanted to know.

"Nope," she said. He let his eyes close.

"Good," he said so soft she could hardly hear. "You can have my stuff and welcome to it," he added. "Just stay with me awhile first." His voice was getting softer and softer. "Just talk to me and . . ." He was unconscious once more. Virginia stood up beside him. Her horses snorted impatiently as she looked at him.

"Darn you," she said (she hardly ever swore). "I'm welcome to your stuff, huh?" She sighed and looked down on him.

"Wiley," she said finally as she knelt down beside him once more, "I fear you are going to be no end of trouble for me."

The man was still alive when she got back to her cabin. Virginia had half expected him to be dead, had in fact expected to take him over to the place of graves and drop him there, only his chest still raised up and fell in rapid little surges.

She felt a little guilty as she noticed a bruise appearing on his forehead, for she had struggled with his weight while getting him into the wagon and dropped his face hard against the wagon bed. His head had bounced on the hard wood, and the reminder of her dropping him was now swelling a little and growing red on his forehead.

Mentally railing at herself for taking this wounded man in, she took him by the shoulders and twisted him around in the wagon bed, then got down and pulled him out the back. She almost dropped him again when his feet dropped from the bed and dragged on the ground, but then she took a better grip on him under the arms. Tugging and pulling, struggling to hold his weight, she pulled him through the door and over to the bed, his heels and spurs leaving two uneven trails behind.

Getting him onto the bed was not easy for either of them, an act she finally accomplished by crawling up there herself, pulling and yanking on him as she did so. Practically exhausted, she sat there on the floor at his feet, watching the rising and falling of his chest as she caught her breath.

He looked mighty uncomfortable, what with his feet flat on the floor out the side of the bed, and in a minute she rose and lifted his feet to the bed. The bed was far too short for his lanky frame and his feet hung over the end, spurs digging into the blanket.

Virginia pulled his boots off, no easy feat in itself, then got a basin of water and a cloth. Now it was time for the part she really dreaded. She rolled his hips onto the right side, then moved his shoulders the same way. Taking her scissors, she cut up the side of his shirt along the seam. She had to cut up the side of his long underwear also, and suddenly his awful wound was open to the light and air.

"Oh, good Lord," she said softly as she looked at the damage the .50-caliber Sharps had done when it blasted out his back. There was splayed-open flesh the size of a small dinner plate crusted with dried blood, and she could clearly see the ends of a broken rib glistening in the meat. She felt her breakfast rise and rushed outside to be violently sick in the grass beside her home.

Reluctantly she went back inside. He had not moved, and was still alive.

"You're a tough old bird for sure," she said to him, surprised he hadn't checked out yet.

Pulling the bandanna from his wound was the worst thing she had ever done in her life. It was stuck, glued into his flesh by his own dried blood. When she pulled it from him, she could actually feel the flesh tear as it stuck to the cloth. The rib ends glistened slippery white in their bed of mangled flesh.

Forcing down her urge to be sick again, she reached into the wound and fit the ends of the broken rib together. They were jagged but all there, and the ends fit together exactly and held in place. Her ministrations had started blood oozing from places on the exposed flesh, and she did not know what else to do for him, so she kept the cloth wet and rested it on his face. She took a blanket and rolled it, wedged it under him so he could not easily roll over onto his raw wound, then sat there and studied the man.

His face was pasty white, and she wondered how long it would take him to die. He was not very old, maybe in his twenties, and he looked almost boyish with his long eyelashes dark on his pale skin. Occasionally his eyes would flutter as he looked at something only he could see, and she wondered what was happening, what he was doing inside his head.

When time passed and it seemed like he wasn't going to die right away, she saw to his horses and the team and cooked some dinner. Every now and then she would come and wet the cloth and lay it on his forehead again, but there just wasn't a whole lot more she could do for him.

She sat and sewed for an hour, until her eyes began to water on account of the poor light, then checked him once more. He was still breathing—barely. She held the lantern by his wound. It was crusted over with dried blood. Probably be a good idea to wrap it in bandage for the night.

She took one of Mom's old petticoats and tore it into strips, then folded one into a pad and placed it against the crusted wound. She tied that in place with another strip. It felt strange to push her hand underneath him as she reached for the bandage; it made him seem more like a real living man instead of just a wounded thing. He never moved or made a sound. He was hurt real bad.

She took a quilt and made herself a bed on the floor in front of the fire. She pulled off her boots and crawled in, then lay there looking at the stranger in her own bed.

"I hope you don't die, Wiley," she said to the motionless lump. "'Specially not in my bed." She closed her eyes and thought about the man.

If he died, she would bury him out with the rest. It would be a lot of work, but she could handle it, and it was the least she could do. He'd told her she could have all his stuff, after all.

It was the other possibility that bothered her most.

If he didn't die, she would be stuck with him until

he got well enough to travel, maybe months. Life was tough enough for one. How would she keep the two of them alive and fed for that long? 'Course, maybe he had some money on him and some food on the pack animal. She would go through his stuff in the morning. He'd likely be dead by then any-way.

Chapter Three

Wiley wasn't right. He didn't feel any sharp hurt or anything like that. He just wasn't right inside or outside either. Everything seemed fuzzy and unreal, as if something was dreadfully wrong, only he wasn't worried. Then it felt like something alive was in his trouser pocket, and that sensation was so weird that he opened his eyes and looked right into the face of an angel.

She was all blurry and out of focus, but she had a halo of light around her head, and she had an expression of infinite compassion. She had no hair and even so, her ears didn't stick out a whole bunch. She had to be an angel. She appeared to be going through his pockets.

Seemed strange that an angel would be going through his pockets, but Wiley had never been dead before and maybe that was normal procedure for angels when somebody new arrived.

''Hello, Angel,'' he tried to say, only it came out muffled and far away. He tried again. ''Hello, Angel.'' Better. Still not perfect though. Everything was supposed to be perfect in heaven.

He said it once more, and this time he could hear

the words and they sounded right and clear and crisp to him. Her eyes widened and swung up to his face.

''Hello, Wiley,'' she said back, and then Wiley was sure she was an angel and he was dead, else how would she have known his name. He allowed his eyes to close and relaxed all over. Being dead wasn't so bad if there were going to be beautiful angels around. Only thing wrong with being dead was that everything felt so fuzzy and unreal. He saw the blackness coming, saw it swallow the glowing light first in a small circle, then swelling until it once more surrounded everything. He was not afraid of the dark. When you're dead, you don't have to be afraid of anything anymore.

Virginia had been carefully going through the man's pockets, trying to be as gentle as possible. It felt really strange, almost wrong, to be going through an unconscious man's pockets. Besides the wrongness of it, there was something a little bit nasty, almost dirty, about touching a man in that part of his anatomy, even when he wasn't aware of the touch. When he spoke, he about startled her to death.

''Hello, Angel,'' he said, almost in a normal voice. Virginia jumped and jerked her hand from his pocket. Nothing in there anyway. Well, almost nothing.

The man's eyes were open and he was looking at her, only he didn't really seem to be inside, like a house with the windows lit but nobody home. Virginia's hands flew up to cover her bald head.

''Hello, Wiley,'' she said, and his face took on a look of peace and his eyes drifted closed once more.

Nobody had seen her bald head since . . . since . . . why nobody had *ever* seen her bald head except her. And now this stranger had. Likely he wouldn't remember, but it made her feel strange that someone knew her deepest, darkest secret. 'Course he wasn't likely to live long enough to tell anybody. She took the cloth, wet it, and gently placed it back on his forehead.

"Angel, huh?" she asked the unconscious man. She did not smile.

The wagon rolled into Big Bear Creek about noon on Sunday. There was a young girl driving, and at first Sheriff Foy thought she was alone. This was unusual enough that he got out of his chair on the boardwalk and walked out to see what was going on. The girl saw him coming and reined the two horses to a halt.

"Howdy," said the sheriff. "You're a little late for church." She looked down on him, expression haggard.

"Church?" she asked. "Today is Sunday, then?"

"Yup," and he nodded. "You got trouble, ma'am?"

"I have loads of troubles, Marshal," she said.

"Sheriff, ma'am."

"Sorry. Sheriff." She indicated the back of the wagon. "I have a sick man in here. Wonder if you can direct me to a place I can stay and nurse him back to health."

"Sick, huh?" Foy asked. "There's a doctor over the livery, if you've a mind to go." She appeared to think about that.

"I believe I would like to get him bedded down somewhere first," she said. "Then, once he is cleaned up good and proper, I can fetch the doctor to see to him." The sheriff thought for a minute.

"Walter Hagan over at the Wooden Bucket has

a shack out back,'' he said. ''I reckon he might be willing to rent it out for a while.'' He didn't tell her that the shack was empty since Walter's last whore had been run out of town by the womenfolk.

The girl looked down the street at the Wooden Bucket Saloon.

''You mean I have to go in there to see him?'' she asked, uncertainty plain in her tone. Sheriff Foy smiled graciously.

''Tell you what, ma'am,'' he said. ''You drive on down there, and I'll have Walter come outside and talk to you.''

''Thank you, Sheriff,'' she said and favored him with a relieved smile.

''Foy, ma'am,'' he said. ''Sheriff John Foy.''

''Thank you, Sheriff Foy.'' She clucked to the team and her wagon jerked into motion once more.

Her purse was lighter by one twenty-dollar gold piece as she stood and surveyed the dusty interior of her new home. Twenty dollars gone forever, and only two months rent to show for it. In other words, nothing to show for it, but she could see no other way to take care of Walter.

She set to work cleaning, leaving Walter sound asleep in the wagon until, by late afternoon, the place had been scrubbed and swept and dusted within an inch of its life. Finally it met her standard of cleanliness, and she went out, woke Walter and helped him inside. He was very weak and dizzy, practically leaning all of his weight on her, and it was a relief when she finally got him seated on the bed.

Katie pulled off his clothes down to his long underwear, and was just getting ready to lay him down, when his bowels rumbled dangerously. Walter got a distressed expression, lurched to his feet and stumbled out the door. Exhausted, Katie sighed and sank down on the bed. Knowing Walter—and after a week of his illness she knew him pretty well—he would be gone for fifteen minutes or so.

She would be glad to get him bedded down. She would be able to clean herself up, then go out on the street to the café and eat with civilized people. She would bring some dinner back for Walter too. He was getting pretty weak. It would do him good to eat some if only he could.

She could hear him out there, even through the closed door.

"Oh, Lord!" he was saying. "Oh, Lord, oh Lord!" over and over. She could hear the other sounds he was making too, and had to wonder where all that nasty stuff came from. Way he was eating, or rather wasn't eating, he should have been plumb empty days ago.

It was fifteen minutes exactly, when the door opened and he staggered back inside.

"Oh, Lord, Katie," he said weakly as he dropped on the bed and allowed her to tuck him under the blanket. "I fear I am dying." She rested her hand on his brow.

"I think not, Walter," she said gently. "Every living thing has a time to die, and I do not feel it is your time yet." He looked up at her with large wet eyes.

"I hope you are right," he said in a voice she had to strain to hear, "but I cannot ever remember feeling so sick in my whole lifetime through."

"Do not worry so, Walter," she soothed. "I shall take care of you until this passes."

"It sure enough should pass," he said with a spark of life. "Darn near everything else has." She laughed a bubbly little laugh.

"I am going to clean up now," she said. "You promise you won't watch?"

"I am too tired to watch, Katie, and that's a fact," he said and allowed his eyes to drift closed.

Katie looked down on the sick man for a long minute, then sighed and straightened and went outside to the pump. She could hear a piano playing inside the Wooden Bucket, and briefly wondered what went on inside a saloon; she wondered why women were not allowed to go in there, least not her kind of woman. She began to pump the bucket full.

There was a moment of silence when she walked through the door of the Railhead Cafe. The tables were crowded with men, although there was one other woman in there eating with her husband. She looked up at Katie, but gave no signal or change of expression.

Another young woman came out from the back. She was pretty, with a straggle of hair stuck to the sweat on her forehead. One eyebrow went up when she saw Katie standing just inside the door.

"Howdy," she said. Katie nodded. "C'mon in. Tables out here are full, but you can come on back to the one in the kitchen if you've a mind."

"Thank you," Katie responded politely, and followed the woman back to the heat of the kitchen. There was an older man, a much older man, tending a steak in a skillet, but he barely gave Katie a glance as she walked through. Across the kitchen was another room with a single table—obviously where the folks who worked there ate. Katie gratefully sank into a chair.

"You'd be the girl with the sick man, I'm thinkin'," the woman said. Katie was not surprised she had been a topic of conversation. Small towns were the same, no matter if they were located in the East or the West.

"That's correct," she said.

"Well, my name's Alice," said the woman. "That man in the kitchen's my dad. Fix you something to eat?"

"Yes, please," said Katie. "My name is Kate Withrow."

"Well you are sure welcome here, Kate," said Alice. "I figured you might be a little more comfortable back here by yourownself instead of out front with all the local louts."

Katie smiled appreciatively. "That was very thoughtful," she said.

"Alice!" boomed the man from the kitchen. "You leave town or something?" Alice grinned.

"Don't let Dad scare you none," she said. "His bark is lots worse than his bite." She went back into the kitchen and in a second Katie saw her lugging a plate loaded with food out to one of the customers out front.

The private dining room was an isle of peace in a sea of cacophony. Oh, she could still hear the banging of dishes, the clattering of plates, and the hot sizzle as slabs of meat dropped into hot skillets, but the noises and the bustle were subdued, as if they were happening far away. It gave Katie a chance to think, a chance to be by herself.

It seemed like eating was going to be a pretty healthy expense, at least until she got set up for cooking in their shack. She wasn't broke; in fact, she was pretty well heeled, but squandering her resources was not the kind of thing she was prone to do. She would have to get busy, maybe get a job. Then she could save the money that had suddenly become hers, save it until there was some kind of emergency. Or until she got married, if she ever did.

Alice came in with two plates on which were piled thick slabs of roast beef with small, red potatoes and green peas. She put one in front of Katie, drew them each a large glass of water from the pump, and sat down across from her. Without ceremony, Alice began to eat.

"Hope you don't mind the company," she said around a mouthful, "but this is where I eat too."

"Don't mind at all," Katie responded. "Matter of fact, it has been a long time since I had another woman to speak with."

Alice took a swig of water. "You're pretty well educated, aren't you?" she asked. Katie smiled.

"My father was a teacher," she replied.

"He the one what's sick?" Alice asked.

"No. The sick man is Walter Donnahue. He saved my life when Father was killed."

Alice raised an eyebrow. "When did all this happen?" she wanted to know.

"Last week," said Katie. "Hadn't been for Walter, I'd likely be dead in the wilderness just like Father."

Alice took a small potato and put it in her mouth. "Tell me about it," she said in a muffled voice. Katie rather suspected that whatever she said would be spread all over town by tomorrow morning, but when she thought about it she couldn't see where that would hurt anything.

"Well," she began, "I was in the back of the wagon and Father was driving. . . . " She didn't mind telling Alice. Katie felt they were going to get a chance to become good friends. She could use a friend. Right now, the only person she had at all was Walter.

* * *

Doc Weber had been tending to the ailments of the locals for near fifteen years. When he had pulled his buggy into town there hadn't been more than three small buildings, and one of them held Mary MaGraw, who was busy engaged in giving birth. Only she was not having an easy time of it, and it was her yelling that prompted Doc Weber to stop in the first place.

There's something about the yelling of a woman in hard labor that a doctor can recognize, something special about the screams that calls to him loud and clear. And so he had stopped and gone in and chased the menfolk out—they had no idea what to do anyway—and set about to doing that which he did best.

The result was David MaGraw, a feisty little red-head, and the fact that the boy had died at ten from consumption said nothing about Doc Weber's skill at delivering babies. It was just said that Doc was not a miracle-man, that he could do what he could do and no more. It said nothing about how Doc had mourned the young boy, and would mourn him until the day he died.

Unfortunately, there were lots of people Doc would mourn, for he knew all too well that medicine was in its infancy. Someday, maybe, doctors would be able to cure some of the awful afflictions the flesh was heir to. Someday, should he live long enough and should the science of medicine learn enough, he would be able to cure the burst appendix, the smallpox, the measles, the consumption. But for now, all he could do was do the best he could do, and watch a lot of his patients die.

Many times he wondered if he was going to be strong enough to hold up under the weight of all those dead patients until it was his turn to slip from the boundaries of human life. It seemed almost more than a man could bear. All those lives, trusting in him. All those lives slipping away to who knows where, leaving behind another empty shell, another symbol of his failure, another burden for his rounded shoulders to bear.

But as little as he knew about medicine, the general population knew even less. So he kept on; he kept on treating the treatable and easing the untreatable into the next world. He had to. If he quit, they would go back to the strange superstitions and weird practices prescribed by stupid people in a misguided attempt to be of service.

When he opened the door to her timid knock, he knew who she was immediately. He had been expecting her.

"Hello, Doctor," she said. She was very young and very pretty, but her eyes looked tired to the bottom of her soul. Tending the sick could do that to a person. Doc knew all about it.

"Hello, young lady," Doc said. "You'll be Katie Withrow."

"Yes," and she smiled. The whole room seemed to light up with her smile. Doc reminded himself to be careful. He couldn't start liking this person too much. Someday he might have to sit helplessly by and watch her die.

"You want me to come and look in on your man," he said. It was not a question.

"Well, he's not my man, exactly," she said back. "He just saved my life and I am trying to do the same for him."

Doc had already heard the story. He'd heard it in the Wooden Bucket when he stopped in for his morning drink. Not that he was a drinker, although he figured he sure had plenty of right to be one if he wished. No. He just took a morning shot to clear his mind . . . and his breath too, come to think of it. Just one shot, then breakfast and business. If there was any business.

"Sometimes we cannot do what we cannot do," he said bluntly.

"That sounds like a quotation from somewhere," she said, "but for the life of me I can't say where." Doc took a second look at the woman. She was obviously educated. That was unusual out here. Unusual in a woman anywhere, come to think of it.

"First said by Doctor Richard Weber," he said. "About fifteen seconds ago." She laughed again.

"Well, it certainly sounded intelligent," she said. In spite of himself, he smiled. What a sucker for flattery he was.

He took his bag and followed her down the stairs and across the street to her home in back of the Wooden Bucket. Doc had been in that house before, both for business and otherwise, but he was not indelicate enough to point that out. The patient was lying in the same bed the Doc had occupied more than once.

"Hello, young man," said the doctor. The young man had that awful look, that look of almost death that Doc had seen too many times.

"Hello, Doc," he said weakly. Doc put his hand on the man's sweaty forehead. There was no fever to speak of. That was always a good sign—at least he thought that was always a good sign. He looked up at the woman who was hovering protectively by his side.

"What's wrong with him?" Doc asked.

"I couldn't say," she replied. "He spends an inordinate amount of time in the outhouse. He complains of severe headaches too."

''I see,'' Doc said knowingly. He had absolutely no idea what was wrong with the man. Sometimes it was like that. Sometimes folks just got sick, just came down with something, and withered away to nothing and then died. Maybe this was one of those sometimes. On the other hand, sometimes folks got sick, withered away to nothing, and then got better. Maybe this was one of *those* sometimes.

He took a bottle of laudanum from his bag. It should do no harm, and that was part of the oath he had taken so long ago. Do no harm. A doctor should be able to cure, not just try not to make matters worse.

''Here,'' he said to the woman, Katie. ''You can give him a couple of spoons of this to make the pain better. Tastes terrible, but he will like the results. Try to get him to eat if you can, and he should drink a lot of liquid. Man with his problem needs to replace all the moisture he is leaving out back.''

''Okay, Doctor,'' she said as if he were some kind of god. Patients treated him like that a lot—until their loved ones died, anyway. She took the bottle from him and set it up on the shelf over the bed as if it were a shrine.

''It's just laudanum,'' he explained. ''Won't really make him better, just knock down the pain.'' She nodded and jerked her head to the side, indicating she wanted to see him outside.

Oh, Lord! Here it came, another out-of-earshot conference with concerned loved ones. How many times had he done that very thing before. How many times had the loved ones listened intently as he destroyed their hopes and their lives. He allowed a sigh to bleed from his insides. Maybe one drink in the morning wasn't enough anymore. He turned to follow her outside.

"Doc," said the man in the bed. Doc turned back.

"Yes?" He could see the woman waiting by the door.

"My feet feel like they're on fire," the man said.

"That's normal," said Doc, not knowing if it was or not. The woman was waiting patiently. They always waited patiently. "You'll be fine. Just take a few days to get over this is all." The look came into the man's eyes. The look of a desperate patient being told what he wanted to hear. They always believed, no matter how sick they were. They believed because they wanted to believe. Maybe if Doc helped in no other way, that dose of peace and trust was enough. He turned and followed the woman outside.

Chapter Four

Cyrus Hanson owned the general store and was likely the most prosperous man in the whole town, not that it was a whole lot of town, leastwise not yet. It was because he was so successful he had been elected mayor. Of course, some of the people voted for him because he was carrying their marker, but some of them who didn't owe had voted for him too, and he was flattered and took the position seriously. For this reason, he already knew about the young, attractive newcomer to his town. The moment she came across the street and through the door, he knew this had to be her.

She was young, maybe sixteen or seventeen, with lovely red-brown hair that gleamed with moving highlights as she came across the street under the bright sun. She was dangling her blue bonnet casually by the straps from her right hand, waving it back and forth absently as she walked, just as a child might do. Her blue dress, while prim and proper, could not conceal the lithe young form inside, and she moved like a healthy young animal, which was just what she was, actually.

Cyrus noticed, out of the corner of his eye because pretty near his full concentration was on the girl, how every man on the street was watching her move toward his store. The looks weren't necessarily lewd or nasty, although doubtless some of the thoughts behind them were, but mostly appreciative as each man looked at this pretty, desirable young woman and measured himself against her, or wanted to.

So entranced was he by the sight that it was almost a surprise when she opened the door and came in and was suddenly standing there face-to-face. Cyrus could smell the fresh soap smell of her.

"Hello," she said.

"Hello, Miss Withrow," he said. Her eyebrow, her right eyebrow, arched prettily upward.

"I seem to have been the topic of conversation," she said.

"Nothing to be concerned over," Cyrus replied. "I'm the mayor, you see. I like to keep up with what's going on around my town." Katie appeared to be suitably impressed with his title. This, of course, puffed Cyrus up a little inside.

"I shall have to be extra special nice to you then," she said and followed up with a cute smile that crinkled up her nose.

"How is your man doing?"

"He is not my man, Mayor," she said. "He saved my life and I am trying to do the same for him, although I am concerned that I may not be so successful as he was." Cyrus had already heard the story.

"I am sorry to hear about your father," he said, and it was as if the clouds came down from the sky and settled in her eyes. The loss of her father had hurt her, and he had hurt her by reminding her. He felt ashamed of himself.

"Thank you, Mayor," she said. "It was an awful waste of a good man." Cyrus could think of nothing to say. "He was a teacher, you know," she continued almost to herself.

"I am truly sorry, Miss Withrow. We could have used a teacher here. Our last one, a lady teacher, left town rather suddenly." That was more than true. Once the women of the town had discovered the teacher was doing a little extra teaching after hours, she had been invited to depart. Some of the young men from her class had not smiled since.

Katie looked at him with interest.

"You mean there is a teaching position available here?" she asked.

"Why, yes," he said.

"How about me taking the position?" she asked, eyes cast down on the floor, almost embarrassed to be asking for employment. Cyrus studied her objectively, or at least as objectively as his hormones would allow. She looked mighty young to be a teacher. In fact, she was more of the age to be one of the older students. She looked up to him eye-to-eye.

"I have quite a bit of experience tutoring students for my father," she said, as if she could read his mind. "I believe in education, and will tolerate no pointless frivolities in my class."

"The pay is only thirty dollars per month," he heard himself say. She beamed at him.

"Oh, that will be fine," she said. "I really only need enough to pay my rent and take care of Mr. Donnahue. We won't eat high on the hog, but I should be able to make do."

"Well," he heard himself drawl. "Maybe we could go forty a month." He couldn't believe he had said that out loud. She clapped her hands together.

"Oh, that would just be wonderful!" She reached out and touched him on the arm, a gentle touch that he felt hard and clean and warm through his puffy sleeve.

" 'Course, I have to get approval from the town council," he said. Her face fell. "No, no. Don't worry," he said. "It is just a formality, I assure you." She looked relieved.

It was like she didn't know her hand was still resting on his arm. He didn't want her to move it, and could barely conceal his disappointment when she took her hand away.

Cyrus turned and went back behind his counter, back where he felt secure and in charge.

"Now," he said, "what was it you came in here for besides a job?" He almost smiled when he thought about how the presence of this young lady was going to affect the young boys in the school, especially the ones who had learned the lessons the last teacher had chosen to teach after hours. She took a scrap of paper from her purse.

"I do have a list," she said, and handed it over. Cyrus studied the list. Nice handwriting, a point in her favor. He glanced up at her young form as she looked around the store. Make that *another* point in her favor.

He bustled around trying to act important. He knew he was trying to impress her, knew it was a silly thing for an old man like him to do, but he just couldn't help himself. He didn't think of himself as an old man, actually. He thought of himself as mature, competent, experienced—only he really wasn't experienced. Not in the way he wanted to be.

The pile of goods rose on the counter until he reached the final item on her list. He set the bag of sugar with the other things, took a piece of wrapping paper and the stub of a pencil, and began to add.

"That's a pretty big order," he said. "Comes to eight dollars and fifty-five cents." She looked a little startled.

"You don't have to pay me right now," he said quickly. "I'd be proud to take your marker, 'specially since you are going to be the new schoolmarm around here." Besides, he kind of wanted her to be in his debt. Who knew where that could lead.

"Thank you, Mayor," she said, "but I do not believe in credit. Neither a borrower nor a lender be. . . ." she added. Her slim hand disappeared into her purse and came out with two five-dollar gold pieces. "I hope you have change," she said.

Cyrus held out his hand and she placed the two coins in his palm, leaving her fingertips there just a split-second longer than necessary. Cyrus didn't know if it was accidental or on purpose, but right away he figured he would not wash that hand for a while. Even when he turned away to get her change, he could still feel the warm buttons of her fingertips in his palm.

She plunked her bonnet on her head, not bothering to tie it, picked up the package, and walked out the door. Cyrus walked over to the door and looked out the window, watching the young lady cross the street and walk back alongside the Wooden Bucket Saloon. In a few moments she was out of sight. But she was not out of mind, least not out of his mind.

"No fool like an old fool," he mumbled and went back to his counter. He could still smell the clean soap smell of her, at least until Bertha Watts came in all sweaty and wrinkled a little later.

Lots of weird dreams. Dreams of hurt and sometimes dreams of an angel, all perfect and hairless. Somehow the soft outlines of the wonderful creature were made more beautiful by the absence of hair. It seemed as if the light was always behind her (the angel was definitely a she), and her form was fuzzy and unclear. He would watch her, mostly when she didn't know he was watching her, through eyes that only seemed to open a bare split, just enough to be aware of the light and the angel. And then he would suddenly be taken by the wearies, and everything would be gone until the next time he opened his eyes a slit and she was there.

Virginia tugged on his shoulder, moving him back onto his side so she could remove the crusted bandage and replace it with a fresh one. The man, Wiley, moaned softly when she moved him, but his eyes were still closed. Sometimes they would open, but she could tell he wasn't really seeing anything so it didn't bother her. Soon as he woke up, if he ever did wake up, she would have to start wearing her bandanna even in the house so he wouldn't see her bald head.

It was just as she feared, the bandage stuck to the raw flesh of his back wound. She didn't want to pull it off, really didn't want to pull it off, but there was nothing else to do. She took an edge of the crusted cloth in her hands and braced herself. She would do it fast, and then it would be over with. She knew he would start bleeding again. She yanked.

The man screamed, loud and hard, and his eyes snapped open wide. He about scared her to death.

She dropped the old bandage and her hands flew to cover her head. But he wasn't looking at her, at least he wasn't seeing her. The eyes were vacant, unfocused, and after a moment they slid shut once more. Virginia bent over the wound.

She felt weakness flood over her and she slumped to the ground. How much horror could there be in one life. How much awfulness could God have in store for her? And why? What had she ever done to deserve . . . and then she caught herself. No. She would not do that. She would not permit herself to slip into the easy softness of self-pity. Life was too hard, and she would have to be just as hard to survive. God, if there was a God, must have plans for her, must have reasons for loading her down with such burdens.

The sun had just set and the western sky was blood red, with brightly lighted wisps of clouds hanging over the horizon. Off to the east, a bright star hung low. It was a beautiful sunset, and she suddenly understood, or thought she understood, that the beauty was put there on purpose, provided to ease the pains of day-to-day living. She could feel the tightness slack off inside her and the loosening of her muscles as she drank in the beauty.

It was a balm for her soul, a much-needed relief for that part of her that was really her. She wasn't really this ugly, hairless body. She was something else, something inside that would grow as she aged and then someday be set free to a place where there was no more ugliness, a place where she would be loved. She watched the red deepen into velvet darkness, heard the first hoot of a distant owl. She sighed, got to her feet, and went inside, closing the door softly behind her.

* * *

''If you drop the hammer on that Colt, I will take my pistol to hand and kill you,'' Steve said flat and plain. The entire saloon was silent and not a person moved lest their movement be taken for interference. At the bar, one of the cowhands stopped as if frozen, a drink halfway to his lips, and it would have been funny if the situation was not so deadly serious.

Marcus Wallers looked down the barrel of his cocked Colt across the table at the young man he had been planning on shooting. The moment of silence dragged out as Marcus thought on the new development, and he could see the sweat beading on his potential target's forehead as the man contemplated the end of his barrel.

The voice that had threatened him was off to his right side, probably coming from that cowhand who was sitting at the table in the corner eating. He hadn't appeared to be paying any mind to the situation, and his sudden interference in what had been a normal chain of events in Marcus's life put a different light on things.

''You are interfering in something that does not concern you,'' Marcus said without looking away from his target. The young man who was his target was scared, but he *was* wearing a gun and would likely go for it first chance he got.

''Always a bad idea,'' came the soft response from the corner.

''How come?'' Marcus asked, stalling for time while his mind raced frantically looking for a graceful way out of this position.

''Cannot abide outright murder,'' came the quiet answer. Marcus could almost hear the click of eyeballs as the motionless spectators looked back at him, waiting for his reply. He could not think of anything to say.

''Prob'ly be best for all concerned if you'd just holster that Colt and sit back down,'' said the stranger. Marcus hesitated, wanting to spin and put a slug into the man. Might be a bad idea though. A man should never tackle an unknown like that unless there was no other choice. Might be that stranger was more than a fair hand with a gun. Matter of fact, that was more than a little likely since he had butted into a situation like he had.

''I said you should holster the Colt and sit down,'' the stranger said, more forcefully this time.

Marcus carefully eased down the hammer on his Colt, then slipped the weapon into his holster. The young man who had been his target jerked to his feet and his hand went down for his gun.

''Hold it!'' warned the stranger in the corner. The young man stopped. ''I am trying to eat supper here,'' said the man patiently, and Marcus turned to look at him. ''I am eating supper and I will not take kindly to anyone doing any serious shooting while I am eating. Don't set right, you know. Killing and supper, I mean.''

The man was maybe twenty-five years old, and his hand was nowhere near his gun. In fact, he shoveled up a forkful of potatoes and transferred them to his mouth while Marcus and everybody else in the place stared at him. He chewed calmly, eyes slowing taking in the spectators. He looked every bit like a common cowhand.

''He was going to kill me!'' said the young man, anger in his voice. The stranger looked at him.

''You don't look a bit dead to me,'' he said, ''least not yet. Now why don't you sit down and stay that way.''

The young man stood there, uncertainty plain on his troubled face. Then he sat down. Marcus stood there, looking at the eating cowhand who was suddenly much more than just a cowhand, at least in *his* eyes. The man chewed slowly, eyes on Marcus. Finally, Marcus turned and walked slowly to the swinging doors, trying to think of something good to say, something that would make people remember him and fear him. Only he could think of nothing. Nothing dramatic to say before he exited, and so he pushed the swinging doors away from him and walked through into the daylight outside.

The doors ''chuffed-chuffed'' closed behind him, and gradually he could hear the saloon come back to life. One man talked, then another, and then a man laughed, and Marcus flushed in anger. Although he had no way of knowing for sure, it seemed like the man was laughing at him, and Marcus took himself very seriously. He expected everybody else to take him seriously too.

He was tempted to go back inside, tempted to go in and face down that nameless cowhand. It would be satisfying to see that arrogant man bleeding and squirming on the floor. But a nagging voice inside told Marcus that the man was too calm, too sure of himself, and the one squirming and bleeding on the floor might very well be Marcus himself. That's when the girl caught his eyes.

She was coming across the street from the general store, package in her arms. Her bonnet was clapped carelessly on her head, giving the impression of a mischievous schoolgirl, and her face was pretty. No, more than pretty, her face was beautiful. She walked with the careless grace of a young girl in the prime of her life, those few short years when her attractiveness was at its peak, when she could drive men's thoughts to distraction merely by being around.

Marcus said nothing, just stood there and watched the young lady walk into the alley, then he walked to the end of the building and watched her go back to the small shack out in back.

She that was her. That was the girl with the sick man.

He suddenly realized his mood had improved. He was no longer thinking of killing anybody, quite the contrary actually. He grinned to himself and stepped out into the alley. Cards and saloons could wait awhile. Funny how just the sight of a pretty girl could improve a man's mood, or at least change it.

Chapter Five

Steve Skobrak finished the last of his potatoes and leaned back in the chair. He sipped at his coffee and watched the door. He was going to have to stop messing in other people's affairs, or one of these days he was going to get himself shot. For a minute there, he had half-expected that man to come back in the door and begin shooting.

The young man whose life he had doubtless saved kept glancing over at him between poker hands, but Steve pointedly ignored him, wanting nothing more to do with him. Most men didn't get ready to kill another man without a good reason, so it was likely that the young man was deserving of being shot in the first place. Young men had a way of becoming more than obnoxious, and this one struck Steve that way. Steve finished his coffee, got up, and went out the back door.

Not that he had to go to the necessary, just that it seemed like a good idea, a way to avoid the young man; maybe it was a way to avoid bumping into that other one, the one he had talked out of the killing in the first place. Sometimes something like that would wear on a man, gnaw at him until he could not think straight and wanted to build himself back up. Going out the back door seemed like a real prudent thing to do.

Marcus walked up to the door and knocked. He could hear motion inside the cabin, then the girl came over and opened the door. Close up she was even prettier than before. Marcus peeled off his hat.

"Hello, ma'am," he said. "My name is Marcus Wallers. I heard how you have a sick man in here and wondered if maybe there was something I could do to help out."

"Are you a physician, Mr. Wallers?" she asked. Her voice was soft and clear, and it reminded Marcus of how long it had been since he had been with a woman. He had never ever been with a woman pretty as this one.

"No ma'am," he said. "I have spent a lot of time in the frontier though, and am familiar with most of the local diseases. Just seemed like I should stop by and maybe help out." He pretended to turn away. " 'Course, if you'd rather not permit a stranger to enter your home . . ."

"No, wait," she said. "I suppose it would be all right. Maybe you can help poor Mr. Donnahue," and she stepped aside. Marcus walked in.

The place was lots cleaner than it had been the other times he was inside, with not a speck of dust to be seen anywhere. There was the smell of sickness in the room, however, and that did have a temporary effect of dampening his ardor. He looked at the man in the bed curiously. He was lying there, eyes scrunched closed in obvious pain.

"Where does he hurt?" Marcus asked.

"He gets these terrible headaches," she said. "Sometimes he complains that his hands and feet hurt. Says they feel like they are on fire."

"Um hmm," said Marcus as if he was thinking. Actually, he had no idea about what was ailing the man. He had no knowledge of medicine of any kind, but it had seemed like a good way to get to know the girl, a way to get into her confidence and get close to her. He wanted to reach out to her and pull her close, wanted to feel her warm and friendly against him. He'd even settle for warm and unfriendly, just as long as he could feel her warm and soft, front to front.

"You must be tired," he said. "Sometimes caring for a sick man can be wearing on a young girl like you."

"I can manage," she said, eyes clouding over. "Have you ever seen this illness before?"

"Pretty dress, ma'am," he said, ignoring her question. Suspicion came onto her face.

"Thank you," she replied flatly. "What do you think is wrong with him?" she asked, moving closer to the door.

"Lot of buttons on that thing," he observed, moving away from the bed. She opened the door.

"I think it would be best if you would leave," she said. Marcus appeared surprised, crestfallen.

"But ma'am," he said, "I didn't mean anything offensive. I was just trying to tell you that you had a pretty dress and that you must be tired and a little lonely because you have been caring for this sick man." He sounded pious and dismayed.

Uncertainty flashed in her eyes. Maybe she had made a mistake. Inside himself Marcus smiled. He was good at twisting words, good at confusing people and getting them to doubt themselves. It was a good trait for a gambler to have. Got him close to lots of women too.

"Do you have any idea what is wrong with Mr. Donnahue?" she asked.

"No, ma'am, I surely don't," he said. "Got an idea what's wrong with you, though."

"There is nothing whatsoever wrong with me," she said, rather haughtily.

"I think you are mistaken," he said. "I think you are tired clear to the bone, and I think you are all alone in this town with no friends." This was all true. Throw the truth at them and it confused the heck out of them. "I think you have need of a friend," he concluded.

Katie looked at his stranger and could not imagine how she had been so foolish as to let him come into her home. Now he was here, and it was most difficult to get rid of him. It was obvious almost immediately that he knew nothing about illness and could be of no help to Mr. Donnahue.

"I appreciate the thought," she said, "but I have no need of a friend right now. If you cannot help Mr. Donnahue, I would appreciate it if you would leave and permit me to get back to tending to him." There, that ought to do it.

"Sure thing," he said, and walked toward the door. "I think you need a friend though, and I think even more, you need a hug." He swept her into his arms before she could even react, and then he was holding her close to him, arms pinned at her side. He dropped one arm low on her body and pulled her hips tight against him.

"What are you doing?" Her voice was frantic. "Put me down at once. I find this very offensive."

"I find this very offensive," he mocked her, holding her against him, feeling her softness tight against his body. "You need a friend, lady," he said with a small chuckle. "Now what could be friendlier than this.'' He moved his hand, and she began to squirm so frantically she almost got away.

Her scream startled him, it was something he had never expected her to do, and over her shoulder he saw the sick man's eyes click open and swing over to the two of them. The man tried to rise in the bed, but was too weak to do anything. The look on his face, a look of awful suffering, was shocking even to Marcus. He had never seen a man that weak who was still alive.

Marcus swung her aside and kicked the door shut. He could not believe what he was doing. Stooping this low was foreign even to him, but it seemed like he had no control, no direct will, just reflexes. Her squirming and wriggling against him only served to inflame him more. She took a breath to scream again, and he covered her mouth with his own, open wide. Katie twisted her head and screamed once more, then things began to happen almost faster than she could keep account of them.

The door burst open and Marcus flinched and then was gone from her, slammed through the door to sprawl in the well-trodden dirt outside. The stranger who had accomplished this strode out the door and stood in front of the prone man, legs spread, hand hovering over his Colt.

''I believe I have had my fill of you,'' he said in a voice hard and cold with anger. To Katie it was obvious the man on the ground had only an instant to live. He was going to be killed, murdered, right in front of her eyes, and it was going to be on her head. She never should have let him come inside.

''Wait!'' she cried. ''Don't kill him!'' The stranger's hand had already started down for his weapon, but it stopped with the gun halfway out of the holster. He remained there, frozen, as he brought himself under control. Marcus looked up at him, eyes wide, knowing he was only a split second away from eternity. A brief moment of sorrow flashed through his mind. There would be no one to mourn his passing, no one at all. Then he snapped back to the moment, frozen lest he precipitate some action.

"Why not?" asked the stranger finally, voice now under control. He asked it as if it were an everyday type of question, not as if a man's life hung in the balance. He asked it as a man might ask the same thing about not killing a snake or some other varmint. When Katie thought about it, the question was a good one. Why not indeed.

If she stopped the killing, this manlike animal on the ground would be free to attack other women and maybe they would not have a savior around as she had. On the other hand, she felt partly to blame, for she had permitted the stranger to enter her home. Perhaps he had mistaken that for her attentions. The blue-steel gun hung there, half out of the holster, hammer partway back under his thumb.

"I do not want you to kill him," she said carefully. "He is not worth the load your conscience would have to bear, or mine either."

"You don't want I should kill him," he said, plain and steady.

"No," she responded. "Please do not kill him."

"We don't look kindly on men who attack women out here," he said, still motionless.

"I understand," she replied. "I should not be able to live with myself if the death of a man was on my conscience."

"Got nothin' to do with your conscience," he said. "Be me what pulled the trigger on him."

"Do not kill him," she said, plain and clear. "I cannot be more clear than that." Marcus lay there, eyes flicking back and forth from one to the other as they discussed the termination of his life. He was siding with the girl, and that was for certain. Never had he felt closer to death.

The blue-steel gun snapped from the holster, the boom seeming extra loud between the two buildings. Katie blinked and jerked in surprise. She saw Marcus's leg snap up, bending the wrong way at the knee as the heavy slug tore through his flesh and smashed his kneecap. Marcus gasped a couple of times in shock, then began to scream, a high-pitched keening sound that bit into her head, a sound she knew she would hear again and again as long as she lived.

The gun slid back into the holster and the stranger stood there looking down on his handiwork for a moment before he turned to her.

''All right, ma'am,'' he said calmly between screams. ''I did not kill him.'' They locked eyes for what seemed to be a long time, then he turned and walked back inside the saloon. She could hear people running to find out what the gunshot was about and who was doing that awful screaming.

Chicken soup. He lay there in the dark and thought about that. Chicken soup. Each breath brought the scent inside him. He could smell the wonderful smell, just like Mom's, only he knew it wasn't Mom's. He was too old to be that kid anymore and Mom was dead, wasn't she?

Yes, she was dead, gone with the pain in her side while he and his brother had watched helplessly. She had been soaked with sweat from her fever, and not quite right in the head anymore, and then she had died. Just like that. One instant there, next instant gone to who knows where. Gone and leaving the two boys behind with a lot of aloneness in them. As the years had passed, the alone had shrunk some, but likely it would never go away all together and sometimes would come back hard and strong—like it did right now, when he smelled chicken soup.

''Mom?'' he said. He didn't know he was going to say it, was in fact surprised when he heard the word come from his lips. Didn't sound like him either, sort of croaky and weak. Now why would he call to someone who had been dead so long? He opened his eyes.

Things were kind of blurry, like looking through a piece of rock candy. He blinked several times, and gradually his vision cleared. He could still smell chicken soup with every breath.

The angel was sitting there, real close to him, and she was holding a bowl of chicken soup under his nose. There was something different about her, something not quite the same as before. The bandanna. She had a bandanna wrapped around her head, a blue one. He wondered why.

''You have a mom?'' she asked. Her voice sounded kind of hopeful, as if she wanted him to have a mother to palm him off on. He opened his mouth to answer, but only a weird croak came out. That wasn't right. He wasn't supposed to sound like that.

She held a spoon of soup to his lips and poured it in. Chicken soup as good as Mom's. Better, maybe. He swallowed and suddenly realized he was starving.

''Am I dead?'' he heard himself ask. She smiled.

''Not a bit,'' she said. Another spoonful.

''I thought I was dead.'' The soup was wonderful. How come he felt so weak?

"Should have been," she said, and continued to feed him.

Virginia could hardly believe it. The man was going to live. Wiley was going to live and she had saved him. For some reason she felt closer to happy than she had felt since her folks died. She didn't know why. After all, only thing she had done was made him so he could go on struggling and fighting for survival just like everybody else. Sooner or later he was bound to die anyway. But it did make her happy—happier, anyway.

"Who are you?" he asked between sips of soup.

"I found you out there," she said. "You told me I could have all your stuff, remember?"

Wiley thought about it. It was coming back to him.

"You didn't want it, huh?" he asked. She laughed, and Wiley wondered at the sound. He was alive, and he had just heard a woman laugh; life was pretty good even if he did hurt all over.

"He shot me with a buffalo gun," Wiley said more to himself than to her. He was lucky to be alive.

"Not right to shoot something and not eat it," she said.

That struck Wiley as funny, and he could feel the laugh bubbling up from inside, but by the time it got to his mouth it was only a small smile. He looked at her while she fed him like a baby. Her eyes were green, honest-to-god green. Nicc eyes. Nice nose. She had a wide mouth, and he always liked that in a woman. She was pretty. There was something different about her face, though, something besides the bandanna.

"What's your name?" he asked.

"Name's Virginia," she said. He was looking at

her intently, as if he didn't ever want to forget anything about her. She wanted to put her hands up to cover her head, but forced herself to continue feeding him.

Wiley finally put his finger on it. She didn't have any eyebrows. Her eyes were lovely, green and all, but she had no eyebrows over them. No eyebrows to set them off. Now, why would a woman do that to herself?

"I thought you were an angel," he said weakly. She barked a laugh.

"Not even close, Wiley," she said. "Not even close." He took in the last of the soup.

"Close enough to suit me," he mumbled, and then, even as she watched, he fell asleep. She sat there and watched him sleep for quite a while, then brushed a stray hair from his forehead and let her hand rest on his head for a moment. It had been a long time since she had felt hair. He stirred slightly and she pulled her hand back as if he were hot.

Four days he had been unconscious, and for two more days he was too weak to move. On the sixth day, just before dusk, he struggled to a sitting position with much grunting and pain, then swung his feet to the floor. He was weaving in this position when Virginia came back inside.

"What are you doing?" she asked, voice angry and afraid.

"Got to go out back," he explained weakly. "Thought I could make it without help. I was wrong."

"I been cleaning up after you for a week," she said. "'Nother day won't hurt me none."

"I am a man, not an animal," he said flatly. "Men don't rightly do what you are asking me to do. Now will you give me a hand or not?'' It was the first sign of spirit she had seen, and it startled her some.

''Don't you snap at me, Wiley,'' she said harshly. ''I am done in and more than a little cranky.'' He studied her for a moment.

''If you don't give me a hand,'' he said in a patient tone of voice, ''what I'm fixin' to do here will likely make you a whole lot crankier.''

She felt the smile break through her weariness and waved a hand at him.

''Okay, okay,'' she said. ''We'll give it a try, only if you get yourself to bleeding again I'm going to whop you with a kettle.''

The trip was the closest thing to hell Wiley had ever experienced. The earth spun around, wavering and unreal. There was roaring in his head and an ungodly weakness the like of which he had never felt before.

He leaned all his weight on the small woman, surprised she could hold him up. She was a lot tougher than she looked, he figured. Each step was pain, but more than that, each step was weakness—overpowering, body numbing, weakness.

He eased his scrawny flanks down on the cool wood, sucking the foul air into his lungs, trying to regain his sense of rightness, his equilibrium with the real world. His gaze locked on a spiderweb in the corner, and he stared at it for almost a full minute before it registered in his brain that he was actually looking at the nebulous thing.

It was a thing of beauty in an ugly place. Parallel strands of shimmering silk orbited around the straight lines thrown out from the center. The spider sat in the center, feet resting on the strands, waiting for the vibrations that foretold the doom of another insect.

It must have been a new web, for there were no encased victims, so it was likely that spider had been working all night in the dark to create this thing of shimmering beauty. But its purpose was far from beautiful. It was there to capture, to hold prey until it could be killed. Beauty, evil in purpose, was maybe not so evil after all.

His breathing evened out as he gradually came back into himself. A bluebottle fly buzzed a jagged line of flight across in front of him and flew directly into the web, where it buzzed and struggled frantically to free itself, but it was already dead except for the dying itself. The spider felt the vibrations and raced over to the struggling fly.

There was no hesitation, no split-second pause while the spider acknowledged that it was about to take the life of another living creature. The spider gave no apparent thought to the act of killing, or the horrible way it went about the process. The spider just did what it was meant to do. And so did the fly, he guessed.

It was about the worst way to die he could imagine—trapped, held tightly by the slimy stuff on the thin strands, struggling frantically.

The awful creator of the web came dashing over and then the fangs pierced flesh and poison was pumped inside to slowly turn the victim's insides to jelly.

But the worst part of it all was the way the victim's life meant nothing to the spider, which was completely oblivious to the frantic struggles and obvious terror evidenced by its victim. To the spider, the fly was a meal, nothing more. Not a life. Not a living thing. Just a piece of meat soon to be digestible soup, a piece of meat that was, thank God, endowed with portability enough to enter the web, but not anything worth mourning. The fly would not be missed.

It was something that Wiley had noticed before. It seemed natural that individual creatures appeared to have little value in the scheme of things. Nature did little to protect individuals. But nature seemed real stingy and protective when it came to entire species.

This single fly would not be missed, and did not make a difference in the overall scheme of things. Neither, for that matter, did the spider. Even when both were gone there would still be plenty of flies, plenty of spiders, plenty of webs. It would be funny if it was the same for humans.

Maybe God, if there was a God, didn't care much about each separate life. Maybe he didn't really care how each life was lived out. Maybe he only cared about the bigger picture, the way the species turned out. Maybe all he cared about was whether they could survive. Maybe he just sat there and watched, as Wiley had just sat and watched the small drama between the spider and the fly. Maybe he didn't care at all. Maybe he wasn't even there.

Wiley struggled to his feet, remembering that the woman was waiting for him patiently just outside the door. He leaned against the door frame until things stopped swimming around in his head, then pushed the door open. The woman came over.

"Took you a long time," she said. She fitted herself under his arm, taking his weight on herself.

"I was figuring out the meaning of life," Wiley said.

She laughed.

"Not any meaning to my way of thinking," she

said. ‘‘Just that living is better than dying, and sometimes I am not too certain about that.’’ They started the long, weak walk back to the house.

‘‘I ain’t too certain about it myownself,’’ Wiley said, ‘‘ ’specially lately.’’

Chapter Six

"You have the job," Mayor Hanson said as he stood there outside her door, twirling his hat nervously in his hands. Katie swung the door open wide and smiled like a delighted child before she caught herself and adopted the more serious and aloof decorum she deemed proper for a new teacher.

"Won't you come in, Mayor?" she asked. "I will put some coffee on and we can talk about my new position."

The mayor was torn. How would it look, him going inside a house with such an unseemly reputation in the company of such a lovely young woman? On the other hand, it was his duty as mayor. Of course there was sickness inside, everybody knew about the man on death's door in there, but not many had seen him, and it would be an interesting thing to talk about later. The illness obviously was not contagious. Curiosity won out over propriety, and he stepped inside.

"Thank you, Miss Withrow," he said, and tried not to appear too nosy or curious as he looked around the single-room dwelling.

Cyrus Hanson had never been inside this place

before, which was probably one of the reasons he was elected mayor in the first place. Not that he was above that sort of thing, just that he was not about to "foul his own nest," so to speak. Cleever was a full thirty miles away, and when he went there on his frequent buying trips, he was not above stopping in the local saloon and partaking of all the pleasures offered inside. Matter of fact, that was mostly the only buying he ever really did in Cleever, but the local folks did not have to know that.

Inside, Katie's place was neat as a pin, although there was the smell of sickness in the air, the familiar sour smell of mustard poultices that the mayor remembered from his own youth. The bed stood over next to the far wall, separated from the rest of the room with a hanging blanket that had been pulled back and tied for easier access to the invalid during the day. The form of her sleeping man—no, not *her* sleeping man, just *the* sleeping man—showed through the blanket wrapped tight around him. His face looked very white, what with the unkempt dark hair against the pillow. Even as Cyrus looked, the man groaned and one arm flopped weakly over the side of the bed. Katie absently went over, almost like an automaton, and gently placed the arm back on the blanket.

"How's he doing?" asked Cyrus. Katie glanced down on the man, then looked back at the mayor.

"Not very well, I guess," she said and sighed. "Sometimes he seems a little better and I am encouraged, then he gets worse again." She looked back at the man. "He is really suffering, I'm afraid."

"Too bad," said Cyrus. "Doesn't seem fair for a man to linger like that. Be better off to just plain get better all the way, or to pass on to his final rest."

"Oh, I hope he doesn't pass on," Katie said. "He saved my life, and I've been working so hard taking care of him. It would be unthinkable for him to die after all that."

"Sometimes we cannot control what the Lord has planned," Cyrus intoned.

"I suppose you're right," she said. "Only he has suffered so much. . . . " She turned away from the man. "I can make some coffee," she offered, "or I have some lemonade I just made this morning."

"Lemonade would be fine," Cyrus responded. He sat on one of the two chairs at the table and watched as she took a glass from the shelf and poured it full. She set it in front of him, then got one for herself and sat down across the small table.

"I got the job," she said.

"Yes," he said and sipped at the lemonade. "The council agreed just as I said they would." He paused a second. "I must tell you they were not pleased with the fact that a man was shot right in front of your house. They were even less pleased when it was revealed that he had been inside."

"I don't blame them." Katie looked crestfallen, embarrassed. "I was foolish to let him inside. It will not happen again."

"I'm sure," said Cyrus in his most imperious voice. Then, because she looked so chagrined, he added, "The schoolhouse is at the end of the street, you know."

"Yes," she responded, raising her eyes once more. "I have seen it. Sometimes I walk in the evening."

Lovely eyes, he thought. Lovely girl. He wondered for a brief moment if the two of them . . . no. Probably not. But at least he had a reason to be with her, to talk with her, to see her. A lot of men would like to change places with him, he knew. He had heard some of them talking about her, about her devotion to the sick man, how pretty she was, how good she was. "A good woman," Gabriel Wote had called her, like it was the rarest thing in the land, and maybe it was.

"The schoolhouse is yours now," Cyrus said, hearing himself speak like a mayor even as he thought like a man. "Since harvest is done, the council wants school to start Monday next."

"Monday?" Katie was surprised. "That only leaves three days to get ready."

"I know. Word will be got out to most of the people with children." He finished his lemonade and carefully set the glass on the table. She rose to her feet, and he realized with some reluctance that their conversation was over.

"I thank you for coming to tell me this," she said. "I had best get over to the school as soon as possible to see what must be done before Monday." She ushered him to the door, and then he was outside looking back at this lovely young woman.

"If there is anything else I can do," he said, "do not hesitate to ask."

"Thank you, Mayor," she said. "Thank you for everything." He heard the man moan behind her.

"You're welcome, Miss Withrow." The door closed and she was gone. The mayor's mood was pensive as he walked alongside the saloon and back onto Front Street. Old Mrs. Tope looked at him coming from alongside the saloon and raised an imperious, holier-than-thou eyebrow.

"Good day, Mrs. Tope," Cyrus said and touched the brim of his hat. He knew what she was thinking, and it irritated him, but he did not let on.

"Cyrus," she bit off his name and swept on past.

Cyrus turned and watched the hefty form stride away from him. He was dismayed to find himself thinking of her as a woman instead of just an obnoxious, annoying witch. He sighed and started across the street to his store. Maybe it was time to do some more buying in Cleever.

The schoolhouse door opened under her hand, hinges protesting slightly at being abandoned for the last three months. Katie could hear the scurrying of little rodent feet as she pushed it open and stepped inside the school. She looked around the single room, assessing its condition. Actually, it was not as bad as she feared.

There were eight small windows, very dirty, two on each wall, through which the late afternoon sun filtered milky light into the room. A stove stood proudly in the corner, and later in the year when real fall set in and winter began to loom, some of the older boys would be assigned to come in early and fire it up so there would be heat.

A sloping shelf ran around three walls of the room to serve as a desk for the boys and girls who would learn here, and a straight bench crossed the center of the room for the younger children. Her own desk (how weird *that* sounded) was high with a tall stool behind, so she could keep a wary eye out for any shenanigans. A ruler lay prominently displayed on the top, waiting for any errant knuckles to smack. The gad, a five-foot, supple hickory sapling, stood in the corner, extending her reach should further discipline be deemed necessary.

Of course, it appeared as though every rodent in the county had been accustomed to using the deserted school as an outbuilding, and a heavy layer of dust covered everything like a thin gray blanket. It was nothing that couldn't be cleaned up with a thorough scrubbing though, a project she would begin the very next morning. Tomorrow would be Saturday, and she had two days to get the school back in order before she would be faced with a roomful of students, her students.

For now, she walked over to the desk that would be her station, then turned and surveyed what would be her province as of Monday morning. It was hard to believe she was about to be a teacher. She knew her father would approve; she could almost feel him smiling down on her from wherever that awful bullet had sent him.

There was a blanket and a small pillow tucked away back there and she wondered what the former teacher could have used them for. Several sheets of paper lay on top of the desk, with the name Simon written on them in flowery hand, over and over again, sometimes in capital letters, sometimes printed, sometimes written, as if the teacher had been keeping her hands busy while thinking about someone named Simon. Gentleman friend, most likely.

Things were not totally primitive, for a blackboard of real slate hung proudly on the back wall. There was no chalk to be found, though. She guessed the last teacher had taken it with her.

Katie walked to the door and looked back. She was going to be spending quite a bit of time in that room from now on. She gently closed the door on its protesting hinges, and walked through the afternoon light back to her home, such as it was; back to her other responsibility, Walter, who was having one of his slightly better afternoons. She would tell him all about her new position if he could stay awake long enough. Maybe he would feel well enough to eat a little. He was getting godawful thin, scrawny almost.

Walter was actually sitting up in bed when she arrived home. His eyes bulged and his skull clearly showed through his parchment-thin skin.

"Where were you?" he asked accusingly. "I wanted you and you weren't here." Katie sighed. Sometimes it was a real burden caring for someone who was so sick all the time. The sickness made him angry and irritable, and he often said bitter and harsh things to her, likely things that he really didn't mean. She tried to look past his rudeness, to see it as a symptom of his weakness and his pain. Still and all, there were beginning to be times when she wished she could be rid of him. Then she would remember the gentleness of her father and the awful way he died, and she would bite back her impatience and care for Walter the way he deserved. It was amazing how much suffering one man could do and still go on living. No wonder he got cranky every now and then.

She helped him from the bed and let him rest his weight on her as she walked him out back to the necessary. He was much lighter now than he had been in the beginning, and she guessed he had lost maybe thirty or forty pounds; he probably didn't go much over 140 pounds right now.

She stood out there and waited for him, watching the sun bleed red color from the horizon as dusk began to fall. She could hear Walter groaning and swearing weakly while she watched the beauty of day's end. Beauty and suffering. That's what life was all about. Sometimes equal parts of each, sometimes more of one than the other, just depending on how lucky or unlucky a person was. Right now, Walter was on the unlucky side of the coin.

Walter opened the door. Katie was waiting for him like he knew she would be. She was always there when he needed her, always there with her gentle hands to place a cool cloth on his brow, or help him adjust his blankets. He put his arm over her shoulder and rested his weight on her. How lucky he was to have her around.

After that long, horrible trip back to the bed, feet burning like fire with every step, he eased back on the pillow and watched her look down on him. Pretty girl, sure enough. If only he would get over this damned sickness, he would want to . . . but the weakness and nausea seemed to come and go in waves. There was something wrong inside him, something dreadfully wrong, and it was just as likely that he would up and die as it was that he would get well, and he knew that was a fact.

"Could you eat something, Walter?" she asked. He could tell she wanted him to eat something, anything. She was worried about him, most likely.

"Maybe something small," he said.

"I'll make you some oatmeal," she said. "I think that may be best."

It sounded awful to him, but he shrugged. Right now all food sounded awful. She went over to the small kitchen area and began to busy herself preparing his oatmeal. He had always hated oatmeal.

Even sick as he was, she was pleasant to watch moving around the small cabin. He reckoned that was maybe the way married men saw their wives, busying themselves with taking care of their own man. Lord, what would he have done without her? Likely he'd be dead and cold by now.

Sometimes he felt very clever the way he had fooled her, but much to his surprise, sometimes he felt a little bit guilty. She had loved her father and he had killed him dead as a doornail without any chance whatsoever. He knew she missed her father, sometimes at night he would even hear her sobbing softly so as not to wake him. He was responsible for those gentle sobs, responsible for making this wonderful young woman unhappy. She was selflessly taking care of him in his desperate hour of need, and he was the one who had made her so unhappy in the first place.

Clever? Or maybe just downright mean. He wasn't rightly certain anymore, but he was leaning toward the downright mean side mostly. It didn't seem possible, but he would take back that bullet if he could, take it back and lift the hurt and missing from her. But he couldn't do it, of course, and he dare not let on that it was him who had killed her father in the first place.

She would doubtless leave him cold if she found out. Leave him cold and all alone and sick unto death. He could not even begin to imagine how awful it would feel to see her go out the door for good, never to return. He felt his eyes flood as he thought about it, and he forced his mind to something else. What had she said? A teacher?

"When do you start?" he asked. He sometimes could hardly recognize that weak voice as his own. What was wrong with him, what was eating his insides away? Maybe it was God's way of getting even with him for all the evil he had done—if there was a God. Seemed like he stood a pretty good chance of finding out real soon.

"I start Monday morning," she said across the room. She turned from the stove, wooden spoon in hand. "I must admit I am excited by the prospect," she said, and smiled like a little girl. Walter's belly twisted in a knot, and for some reason her smile made him angry.

"You ain't smart enough to be a teacher," he said through clenched teeth. Gradually the spasm died away and he could relax once more. Now, why did he say things like that to the only person who had ever been so nice to him? "You are still just a child," he added in an attempt to soften his words. Her smile vanished as if he had wiped it off with a cloth.

"I am not as dumb as you think I am, Walter," she said. "My father was a teacher, and I learned a lot from him."

Her father again. Walter was sick of hearing about her father, teacher or not.

"He was a learned man," he said. "You are just a foolish young girl." It was like he had no control over what he said to her, like he was outside listening to his own mouth say such awful things to her. He endured her gaze as she studied on him for a bit.

"You do not mean to be so hateful, Walter," she said gently. "I believe that is your illness talking, not you."

"Maybe I am a hateful man," he heard himself say. "Maybe I have done enough bad things in my life that you should hate me." She smiled at him, a gentle beautiful smile, and that made him angry too. He struggled to maintain his control.

"Don't you never get mad?" he asked. "Don't you never scream and holler and throw things? It just ain't right, a girl who don't get mad. Just ain't human." He slumped back against the pillow and endured yet another of those maternal gazes.

"Certainly I get angry," she said as if speaking to a child. "Only I know you don't mean those awful things you say to me. I know it is the sickness talking.'' She turned back to the stove. ''After all, Walter, what would you do without me, right now.'' It was not a question, and Walter lay there and thought about it.

She was right and they both knew it. What would he do without her, indeed.

''I'm sorry,'' he heard himself say, and hated himself for it. ''I don't know what makes me go off like that.''

She scooped a spoon of oatmeal into a bowl, stuck a spoon in it, and brought it over.

''Here, Walter,'' she said. ''Try and eat this.'' He looked at it balefully.

''Ain't hungry,'' he said.

She smiled and sat down on the bed.

''That's okay, Walter. I'll help you.'' She held a spoon to his lips. Walter opened his mouth and took the clotted stuff in.

Chapter Seven

Katie's step had an extra bounce as she walked to the schoolhouse, cleaning pail in hand. Walter had seemed to be even better this morning, and she had seen the hope in his eyes, hope that he might be on the road to recovery. This had happened before, that small glint of hope in his eyes, and it only served to make it all the more devastating to him when he suffered one of his inevitable relapses.

But she chose not to think about Walter this morning, for she had work to do, things to do with her hands that would keep her busy, productively busy, for the rest of the day. Her school awaited her ministrations. Her school. How proud Father would have been. The door opened under her hand, squeaking softly. She reminded herself to get some oil at the store and oil the hinges.

In short order, dust motes spun crazily in the window shafts of morning light as she wiped it from the desk and benches, then swept it out the door in a billowing cloud of white.

There were two overgrown paths out back, one to the necessary, the other to the pump. A harmless grass snake slid from the path almost directly underfoot, startling her and setting her heart to beating faster. She watched it twist through the grass and then it was gone, but she walked slower and more carefully after that.

The pump stood like a rusty sentinel over the weathered wooden boards covering the well. Katie brushed away the cobwebs, grabbed the rusty metal handle, and began to pump. Apparently the leather washers inside had remained moist, for it required only nine or ten pumps before she could feel the weight of water, and then a stream of crystal-clear water surged from the spout into her pail.

Katie lugged the heavy thing back inside to find a couple standing there, the man nervously twisting his hat in his hands.

"Hello, Miss Withrow," said the lady. "We're the Rogersons from the gun shop. You'll be teaching our daughter, Ellen, and we are here to help."

"I'm pleased to meet you," said Katie, and she was. A little help would be greatly appreciated. Without wasting words, the two women began to wash down the inside of the schoolhouse. Mr. Rogerson went outside and prepared to start painting a new coat of red on the faded walls.

They worked in silence for a few minutes, then Katie heard a slight cough from the doorway. Another couple stood there.

"Howdy, Miss Withrow," said the man. "We're the Davies and you'll likely be teaching our son, Robert." He shuffled his feet a little. "We're fixin' to help if you'll have us," he said.

Katie went to the door to greet them, and over their shoulders she could see several other couples coming down the street.

"Morning," from the next. "We're the Mapes and you'll be havin' our son, Richard."

''Hello. We're Roger and Agnes Hoole. Our son, Paul, will be in your class.''

''Howdy from the Smithes . . .''

''Morning from the Horns . . .''

In what seemed like no time at all, there were many people bustling around the schoolhouse. There was conversation and storytelling and laughter, but these were people used to hard work, and that's what they did.

The women scrubbed down every inch of the interior; outside some men cleared the paths out back and scythed down the overgrown grass while others completely painted the school. Katie could hear the thumps as firewood was split and stacked neatly by the door.

The women had brought food enough for all, and lunch was a happy gathering as they accepted her into their community, joked with her, and permitted her to listen to and participate in their friendly conversations. Katie was happier than she had been for a long time. Several of the women made her a gift of the leftovers, carefully wrapping the chicken in white towels for her to take home.

Then it was back to work, and as the afternoon wore out there were suddenly fewer and fewer things that needed doing, and then it was almost suppertime and they gathered out front, finished with their labor.

Katie thanked them, promising to do her best teaching their children, and was sorry as they turned and made their way back to their own lives. She felt a sudden loneliness as they left, but she also realized that they had opened the door for her and given her the opportunity to become a part of their community. It all depended on her performance as the teacher of their children. That, and her reputation, for these were hard people, and although they would give her a chance and welcome her if she did well, they would coldly dismiss her and never forget nor forgive should she make another error in judgment.

Her school practically glistened with its new coat of red paint. Mr. Rogerson had even painted the window frames a nice shiny white, and the spotless windows glistened in the fading sunlight. With no small reluctance, Katie turned and headed back home. It was on the slow walk that she realized that for an entire day, the first since the death of her father, she had not thought much about Walter.

''Where you been?'' he asked in a harsh tone. ''I been hungry all day and you wasn't around at all.''

''Sorry, Walter,'' she said. ''Normally you don't eat anything. You appear to be a bit better today.''

''I feel a bit better,'' he said. ''I need to eat something, though. Got to get my strength back, you know.''

''I have some chicken here,'' she said, indicating her cloth bundle. ''Just take me a minute to set it out for you.''

''Good.''

''You feel up to some coffee tonight?'' she asked.

''Sure,'' he said. ''Why not.''

Katie bustled around, putting the chicken on one of their few plates. She took it over to Walter along with a glass of water she pumped, then set about building up the fire in the stove.

She watched Walter eat from the corner of her eye as she pumped the pot full and set it on the stove to boil. Walter was tentatively picking at a chicken leg, taking the food in carefully, as if afraid to completely trust his traitorous digestive tract.

He looked like a mere skeleton of a man, bones

showing clearly through his skin. His temples moved with each chew, and for some reason watching him eat almost nauseated her. She hoped he would not eat all the chicken, and the careful way he was going about it seemed to indicate that there would be plenty left for her.

It would be nice if he went to sleep right after supper, for it was her plan to spend the evening making chalk for that sparkling clean blackboard waiting for her at the school.

Finally he tossed the leg bone back on the plate.

"That's enough, I think," he said, and handed her the plate. There was plenty left for her. Walter eased back down in the bed, wiping his greasy hands on the blanket.

"Coffee," he said.

"Be done in a few minutes."

"I feel better."

"That's nice."

Walter lay back and watched her as she sat at the table and began to eat. She used a knife and fork to pick the meat from the chicken. That seemed like the long way to get the job done to Walter, but he said nothing. It was glorious not to have that awful burning of his hands and feet, not to have that awful sickness deep inside. Even his splitting headache seemed to be easing up some. Maybe this time he would get better, and life could go back to normal.

'Course, he was stuck with this girl/woman now, and couldn't even imagine what life would be like without having her around to take care of him. Might be kind of nice really, what with her making money now, money that would likely be enough to keep a man in whiskey and poker and such. No wonder some men got married.

His stomach twitched with the unfamiliar load of

food, and he analyzed the sensation carefully. No, it wasn't sickness, just fullness. He gave a small sigh of relief. It was not real good for a man to have to keep such close track of his insides like that.

He watched Katie take a couple drops of water from the pump and sprinkle them in the coffee to settle the grounds before she poured him a cup. She brought it over.

"Here you are, Walter." She carefully handed it to him. He sipped carefully. It was plenty hot.

"Once I am well," he said, "it is my intention to show you how to make a good cup of coffee." She looked at him for a moment.

"My coffee is not good?" she asked. Whoa. Maybe he'd better lay back on her for a while. No doubt she would put up with anything he wanted to throw at her, but a man who is busy relying on someone for his every need would do well not to be *too* much of an annoyance.

"Sure it's good," he said. "Just a little bitter sometimes. You put chicory in there or something?"

"No I don't." Maybe he had hurt her feelings a little.

"Maybe it is just my broken taster, then," he said. There, that should remind her that he was a sick man. She looked down on him for a moment.

"If you would like to show me a better way to make it, I will be happy to learn," she said. "I don't drink coffee, you know, so I don't know how it's supposed to taste. It all tastes bad to me." She seemed tired, likely from working all day getting her school cleaned. Walter drained the cup.

"Don't take it so hard, Katie," he said. "Your coffee is good as anybody else's. Except my own." She looked a little mollified. He handed her the cup.

''I'd be pleased to have another,'' he said, more to convince her than anything else. She got another cup and gave it to him.

''You sure you should drink this?'' she asked. ''I don't think too much coffee is good for a man's stomach.''

''You are just a foolish girl,'' he said. ''What do you know about men's stomachs?'' he said as he sipped.

''My father used to drink only one cup a day,'' she said, very sober. ''He said it wasn't good for a man to drink more than that.''

Walter sipped in silence. There it was again, that reference to her father. Every time she brought him up, Walter felt a little tug of his conscience. Likely it was because she was working so hard at taking care of him, and him being the murderer of her father. It was remarkable on account of he had never felt any guilt for any of the others he had killed. He didn't like guilt much, either.

''I wish you wouldn't talk about your father all the time,'' he said carefully.

''Why not? I want to remember him. He was a good man and I loved him a lot.'' Katie had finished the dishes and was setting up the table to make chalk. She took two pieces of board about two feet long and set them side by each as Walter watched.

''I just feel bad when I think of the end he come to,'' Walter said. Her face clouded up.

''So do I, Walter,'' she said. ''Those who killed him had no idea what a good life they were wasting.'' She shook her head as she measured one part wheat flour to five parts of Paris white into a bowl. ''Savages,'' she said as she added a small amount of water to the mixture and began to knead it into dough. He could think of nothing to say to that. Savages. If she only knew.

Katie put several lines of the tough dough on one board, then took the other and slid it back and forth on the first, rolling the lines into round pieces that would dry into chalk. Walter found the process fascinating.

He finished the coffee and handed her the cup. He could feel the warm liquid sloshing around in his belly uncomfortably. Maybe she was right. Maybe one cup would have been plenty.

Being a doctor had lots of drawbacks. A man got to see all the pus-filled, oozing problems the flesh was heir to, listen to women scream in pain and men too, sometimes, and see all sorts of bodily fluids gushing or oozing, each with its own distinctive awful smell. But the worst by far was the sound of that darned knocking on the door in the middle of the night.

The middle of the night was when a man was supposed to hide in the folds of sleep. It was the time for those big-eyed night creatures to rule the world. It was not the time for a man to be jolted from his velvet rest and pushed rapidly into the awfulness that was sickness or injury.

Doc Weber rolled from his bed clad only in his long underwear.

"I'm coming," he called, and fumbled for his trousers. There was another series of loud knocks.

"I said I'll be right there!" He buttoned his trousers and stumbled barefooted to the door, suspenders flopping at his sides. It was Katie Withrow, and her face was serious. She stepped in without waiting for an invitation.

"Worse, huh?" asked Doc Weber. She nodded.

"Worst I've ever seen," she said.

"So what happened?" Doc asked as he took his shirt off the chair and slipped it on. Despite the obvious emergency, rules of decorum still applied and he turned away from her to tuck in his shirt.

"He ate some supper tonight for a change," she said to his back, watching the man miss a flap of his shirt in the back. About half an hour ago he woke up screaming, and he's been squirming around and yelling and crying ever since. She lowered her voice and her eyes. He has been to the necessary twice already," she said. It wasn't something she liked to talk about, especially to a man.

"So what did he eat?" Doc asked.

"He had some fried chicken," she said. "That's all." She hesitated. "We got the chicken from the folks who helped me clean up the school today, so I had some too," she said. "I feel fine. Couldn't be the chicken was bad."

"Man shouldn't eat fried food with stomach trouble," Doc said, just like he really knew what was going on. If you don't know, don't let *them* know you don't know. A good philosophy for a doctor, he believed.

"Can we do anything to help him?"

"Dose him up good with laudanum," he said. His suspenders snapped on his shoulders, and except for his bare feet, he felt dressed. For some reason being dressed always made him feel more competent as a doctor.

"I gave him three spoons of the stuff. Will you come and see to him?" Katie pleaded. Doc sighed.

"Nothing I can do for him," he said. "Most likely he's out cold after three spoons of laudanum anyway."

"I hate to see him suffer like that," she said. "Surely there must be something you can do."

The doc looked at her seriously. Looking at her was not much of a strain on him. Even in the middle of the night she was darned pretty.

"Look, Katie," he said. "Sometimes, no matter how much we want to help someone, it is not in our ability to do so. Sometimes all we can do is make them as comfortable as possible." He sighed. He was giving her good advice that he had acquired through a lifetime of frustration. "Sometimes," he went on slowly, "men are meant to die. Sometimes women are meant to die." Another sigh. "Sometimes even children are meant to die, and there is nothing one human being can do about it. Nothing at all."

She looked him directly in the eye.

"You are saying he is going to die for sure?" she asked.

"I think he is," Doc said. "I don't see much chance of him ever getting out of that bed again, least not for good." He saw her frown and went on before she could speak. "I think he has something inside, something that is eating away at him. A cancer maybe." She drew back at the mention of cancer. Everybody drew back at the mention of cancer.

"But he saved my life," she said.

"I know, and I'm sorry as I can be that you cannot help him. Whatever is eating at him will likely torture him for a while longer, and when he dies it will seem a blessing to everybody. Cancer is not a pleasant way to die." And Doc had seen them all.

"Maybe if I work harder I can save him," she said desperately. Doc gave her his kind expression, the one he had used so many times before.

"You would likely not be doing him any favors

by being heroic and stretching out his life a whole lot,'' Doc said. ''To my way of thinking, there is a time for being alive and a time for dying. Stretching out the time for dying just means that a body has to suffer more before the final peace comes, if you know what I mean.''

He watched her eyes for the look, that look he had come to know so well. Gradually, it came over her too, just as it had so many others: acceptance, reluctant acceptance. Medical science had spoken. If only they knew just how limited medical science really was. Medical guessing would be more accurate.

''You can make it easier on yourself,'' Doc said. ''You have to think of him as not being of this world anymore. He is not like the rest of us. He is half here and half somewhere else, and pretty soon he will step all the way over to the other side and you will be able to get on with living *your* allotted span on this earth.''

Katie stood there and looked at him, this man of medicine. Doc endured her look. He was used to it. He was supposed to be so smart, so helpful, but he knew that he was really just a man, just a scared man who didn't know anything more than anybody else, at least not about the *really* important things in life. Why did they expect him to be so smart?

''I can't give up,'' she said. He looked at her with real compassion this time.

''I know,'' he said, and she turned and walked down the stairs.

Doc closed the door softly. She was so good, almost noble. She wanted to help that man so much, and she could do nothing. He could do nothing. She impressed Doc clear down to the core of his being. Too bad there had not been a woman like that around when he was a little younger, back when he still had hope for the future, for mankind, and for himself. The man who got her would be getting a prize worth keeping and cherishing forever.

Doc sighed and looked over at his bed, still rumpled from earlier. He slipped his suspenders off, knowing that his warm sleep was gone for the night. From now on it would be fitful at best, stuttered with brief twilight images of that man being eaten from the inside and once in a while an image of a young woman, a very good young woman.

Katie stood in front of the school, took a deep breath, and rang the big hand bell five or six times. The clear peals stopped the activities of the children scattered around outside and they began to file toward the door. She could see a larger boy sprinting toward the school from farther down the street.

Katie turned and went inside to stand at the front of the room. It was the beginning of Day One as a teacher. It still sounded strange to her. It still seemed as if she belonged out there with the youngsters rather than up in front in charge.

The children filed in in respectful silence, taking seats on the long wooden bench facing inward. They ran the gamut from about six or seven to young men and women about fifteen years old. When the last child was inside and the door closed, Katie cleared her throat.

"My name is Miss Withrow," she said. "I do not know your names yet, but I shall before the week is out. For now, we will have to make do with very impolite pointing. When I point to you I expect you to rise and give your Christian name." She had their complete attention. "Which of you is the eldest?" she asked. The oldest boy raised his hand.

He was a farm boy for sure, face tanned and lean.

Even his baggy clothes could not conceal the hard muscles of youth. Someday he would be a handsome man, and Katie could see the young ladies looking at him while trying not to be too obvious about it. She nodded at the lad who stood.

"My name is Simon Quent," he said.

Simon. The name that was written all over the last teacher's papers. Suddenly Katie realized what had happened to the last teacher and was appalled at the woman's weakness. Her own student—and not much more than a mere child, either. It never occurred to her that she was only a year or so older than Simon. She put the thought behind her and concentrated on communicating with these children, *her* children for most of the day.

"We shall begin each day with a reading from the Bible," said Katie. It was the way of her schooling. It would be the way of theirs. "Simon will begin today," she went on, "but each of you will get an opportunity." The kids watched Simon come to the front and take up the Bible. He looked at her, query in his eyes.

"We shall begin at the beginning," she said. He opened the book.

"In the beginning," he intoned, reading slowly. "In the beginning . . ."

The door opened suddenly, and Simon stopped in midsentence. The figure of a boy was silhouetted against the bright sunlight. He stepped in, and the form of a man stood there for a moment, then also came inside. With a start, Katie recognized the stranger who had come to her aid that day two weeks previous, the man who had so ruthlessly and casually destroyed her attacker's leg.

She had thought about him often since then. What kind of man could do something so callously to another man? What kind of man would, with a twitch of his trigger finger, send another man into relentless agony, then calmly survey his handiwork with no more emotion than a carpenter examining a board?

Not that she wasn't grateful. What that evil man Marcus had in mind was horrible, to be sure. That he deserved to be stopped and punished went without saying. But this stranger had done all that with such an economy of moves, with such unfeeling relentlessness, and that was what really bothered her about him.

It was the coldness of it all, the emotionless attitude, the carelessness with another human life that really bothered her. Maybe she wasn't quite ready for the western frontier. Maybe she wasn't quite hard enough to survive out here.

Then the man stood in front of her, hat in hand.

"Morning, ma'am," he said. His gray eyes caught hers and held them. Last time she had seen those eyes, a man was screaming in agony in the background. Katie's eyes flicked down to the evil blue-steel gun hanging at his side, then back to his face.

"Good morning," she said firmly.

"This here is my brother's boy, Alfred," he said, indicating the lad standing there. Me and David—David's my brother—figure the boy can do with some schooling when we can spare him from the ranch." Katie tore her eyes away and looked at the boy.

"Hello, Alfred," she said. The boy stood straight and tall and looked her in the eye even though it was plain he did not want to be there. He was maybe fourteen years old and likely did the work of a full-grown man. It was easy to see some of his uncle in the boy's face and attitude.

"Howdy, ma'am," he said.

"My name is Miss Withrow," she said, "Miss Katherine Withrow." She knew she repeated it for the benefit of the boy's uncle, and wondered for an instant why she did that. "You had any schooling before, Alfred?"

"Not much, ma'am," he said. "Been working, mostly." Plain, strong, and honest. Those were good signs in a lad.

"Fine, Alfred," she said with a smile. "Why don't you go sit on the end there, and we'll get you started."

"Yes, ma'am." He went to the indicated seat and sat down. Simon, seated next to him, looked at him curiously, and after submitting to a moment of examination, Alfred looked back coolly.

"Sorry about the boy being late today," the man said. "Won't happen again 'less we need him real bad at the ranch." Katie nodded. That was the way it was with a lot of the kids. Schooling came second, after the work was done.

"All right Mister . . . ?" she said. It occurred to her she didn't even know this man's name.

"Sorry, ma'am," and he actually looked embarrassed. "Name's Skobrak, Steve Skobrak."

"How do you do, Mr. Skobrak," she said. It was amazing the power a teacher had in her own school. The man was actually embarrassed, clearly wanting to escape at the soonest moment. It was all she could do to avoid smiling at his discomfort. "I'm certain Alfred and I will get along fine."

"If you have any trouble with him, ma'am, why you just mention it to me or Davey and we'll see to it," he said.

"I don't doubt that, Mr. Skobrak," she said. "I've seen you in action." He looked at her, eye to eye for a moment, face serious, then turned and headed for the door.

"I'll be going now, ma'am," he said over his shoulder.

"Mr. Skobrak?" she said to his back. He stopped at once.

"Thank you, Mr. Skobrak," she said to his back. He hesitated a moment, then turned back toward her.

"For what, ma'am?" he asked.

"For bringing Alfred," she said. He shrugged.

"Boy needs to know readin' and writin', I figure," he said.

"Thank you for the other day too," she said. Once more there was that serious expression as his eyes held hers.

"You are welcome, ma'am," he said. Then the door closed behind him and he was gone.

Chapter Eight

Steve Skobrak rode along, horse cantering in that effortless movement that ate the distance between town and the ranch. In forty-five minutes, he was swinging in front of the house.

"Davey?" he called. No answer.

The house was empty. But it wasn't supposed to be empty. There was no reason for Davey to be gone, not with all the never-ending work to do. Steve stood there for a moment in the front room, almost afraid to make his next move. There *was* one possible explanation, one reason Davey could be gone, but Steve didn't want to believe it.

He went into the kitchen, pulled down the flour bin, and checked inside. It was gone. All the money, all forty-three dollars, was gone.

He slapped his hat on his leg. "Darn!" he said. It wasn't often that he swore like that. "Darn!" he exclaimed once more, then turned suddenly and went out on the porch. His horse stood there ground-tied, watching him. After a moment, Steve mounted up and headed back toward town.

"C'mon, Lopez," he said to his horse, who was not real anxious to leave home again having just got there in the first place. A nudge with his spurs was enough to convince the reluctant animal, and they moved off, retracing the path they had just taken.

Steve cast back and forth, across the road and into the prairie on each side. Sure enough, about ten yards to the north of the road he came across the tracks of Davey's horse. Davey had kept off the road so Steve wouldn't see the tracks on the way back from school. Another nudge with the spurs and Lopez moved into a fast canter.

Steve's face was hard as he rode. Two months' work. All the fence building and horse catching, all the horse breaking and ranch repairing, all the pleasure and peace of the last two months was wrapped up in that money. Worse, all the trust he had built up in Davey was now as fog in the wind, gone and not likely to return. Some leopards could not change their spots, seemed like.

Town was still thirty minutes away. Too much time.

Wiley grimaced as he eased down on the chair at the table. It was his first attempt at sitting up like a man for his supper. It seemed like weeks since he had been able to stay upright, and he was kind of ashamed at how long it was taking him to heal.

''Feels kind of strange to be settin' here,'' he said. Virginia favored him with a smile.

''Surprise to me too,'' she said. ''I figured you would'a been buried outside long time ago.'' She turned back to her work, dishing out the food onto Mom's old china.

She knew he was watching her; she could almost feel his eyes pressing against her back as she worked. He always watched her, seemed like, and it bothered her some. Of course, she had taken to keeping herself covered all the time now, not like when he had been unconscious, so he would have no way of knowing about her hair, or rather her lack of it. Still, she could feel his eyes. And she wished he would not look at her so much.

She set the plates on the table and poured water into the glasses, then sat down opposite him. When she raised her eyes he was looking her straight in the face.

''Dig in,'' she said. ''More you eat, quicker you'll heal up.''

His eyes dropped to his plate, and he began to fork the food into his mouth, glancing up at her occasionally. Virginia began to eat too.

''I am not going to die,'' he said finally, taking a sip of water.

''My cooking isn't *that* bad,'' she retorted. He let out one of his infrequent laughs. It was a nice sound.

''Wasn't talkin' of your cooking. Meant I am not going to die from my wound.''

''Doesn't seem likely anymore,'' she agreed.

''It's all your fault too,'' he said right back, voice accusing.

Virginia looked him in the eye, caught the twinkle, and smiled.

''Next time I find fresh meat on the prairie, I will gut it right away for certain,'' she declared, and his face split in a broad smile. Lord, how she loved it when he smiled. It seemed to brighten up the whole cabin and made her feel warm and safe somehow.

He took another bite, chewing absently. ''I don't rightly know how to thank you,'' he said, a little too casually, and she knew it was important to him.

''A whole lot of money would be nice,'' she said and smiled. He knew she wasn't serious.

"A whole lot, huh."

"Bunches and bunches," she said.

"What would you do with bunches and bunches of money?" he asked. "Great venison, by the way," he added and proved it by taking another bite.

"Thank you," she said, pleased that he liked her cooking. She thought about the question.

"Be nice to have a big house somewhere," she said. "Be even nicer if it was full of servants who would wait on me hand and foot." He looked at her for a moment, then shook his head.

"You wouldn't like that at all," he said flatly. "You don't exactly strike me as the prissy type." She grinned a big grin.

"Try me," she said. He laughed and shoveled in another bite. His face grew serious as he chewed.

"How come you are living way out here by yourself?" he wanted to know.

"Mother and Father are buried on this land," she said. "I did not choose to leave them." She said it simply, with great dignity, and Wiley nodded.

"I see," he said.

"Once you are better," she asked, "are you still going to be a lawman?" His eyes hardened, and his expression turned cooler.

"I am going to find the man who shot me," he said flatly. "That comes first. Before anything else."

Virginia felt the shock of aloneness at the mention of him leaving. It surprised her, she who had been so used to living alone, so used to staying hidden. Now she had allowed herself to become attached to another human being, and of course he would be leaving.

"I suppose you won't be going until you are

completely healed,'' she said. It was stated as a fact, not a question. He could not know how frantic she was feeling inside, how desperately she wanted him to say he would be staying around. Every day was so much like a treasure for her. Every day was a day when she wasn't alone, so awfully alone.

Wiley was surprised at the coldness of her tone and wondered what he had done to upset her. Seemed almost like she wanted him gone.

'' 'Course, I shall leave at the earliest,'' he said. It's not fair to impose on you any more than I have already.'' He watched her face cloud up, just as a child's might. He couldn't imagine what was troubling her. It had to be him, had to be his staying even longer.

''I would go right now if I could,'' he said, trying to ease her mind.

Virginia looked across at him, trying not to let her devastation show. She remembered what it had been like before Wiley, what it had been like to come home to an empty house—things silent and unchanging, nobody to worry over and care for, and nobody to care for her, not that he *did* care for her. Obviously he didn't, or he wouldn't be talking like that. She got up.

''Sooner the better,'' she heard herself say. She wanted to say more, wanted to curse him for hurting her so brutally, wanted to blame him for her sudden sharp pain. But it wasn't his fault. Not really. ''Sooner the better,'' was all she said and then she quickly turned away so he couldn't read her face. She didn't see the quick flicker of pain cross his face, and for the first time in a long time, his pain was not physical.

The hard silence drew out as she cleaned up the dishes and he sat there and sipped at his coffee.

Dishes done, she went out into the blood red sunset and saw to the animals one last time before night set in hard. She stood there in the little barn, the sound of horses moving around her, and watched the glowing orange orb of the sun slide below the distant hills. Then it was dark and there was nothing for it but to go back inside, back in to the man who had so casually hurt her.

She walked slowly across to the house, took one last look around, and went inside. She pulled in the latch string behind her.

''Howdy,'' said Wiley as if she had been gone a long time. She gave him a half-hearted smile. He was still sitting at the kitchen table, but in the lamplight she could see creases in his face from where he had been resting his face on his arms.

''How come you didn't go back to bed?''

''Figured I had kept you out of your own bed long enough,'' he said. She could see the tiredness in his eyes. ''Figured I would sleep on the floor from now on and you could have the bed.''

Virginia studied the weary man for a long minute.

''If that's what you want,'' she finally said, and began the already familiar process of making a bed on the floor. Steve began the long painful trip out back, just like he always did before night, only this time he slipped his pistol from the belt by the door and took it with him. He *was* getting better.

Virginia straightened and looked after him as he closed the door. She looked for a long time before she sighed and bent to her task once more.

When he got back, Wiley carefully eased himself down onto the makeshift bed and pulled the blanket up to his chin. He eased his head back on the rolled-up blanket she had been using for a pillow. His eyes slid closed and he groaned softly.

Virginia stood looking down on him. Even though he was a grown man with a wild scraggly beard that hadn't been shaved since he arrived, he struck her as a little boy. Maybe it was the complete relaxation, or maybe it was the lack of wrinkles on his forehead now that the pain was gone. She didn't know or care. She knew she loved this man and wanted him around and did not want to lose him.

She took the lamp over to the bedstand, crawled into the bed for the first time in weeks, cradled her hand over the lamp chimney, and blew it out. Soft darkness settled over the room. She could hear his breathing and suddenly realized she could smell his smell in the pillow; it was a nice smell, a man smell. Her eyes welled full and she squeezed them shut, feeling the strangeness of two tears sliding on her cheeks. She had never even cried when her parents had died, but now she was crying over losing some stranger. Heck, he wasn't even gone yet!

Inside she knew that it was silly for her to love him. He was the first man she had been close to in years. *That* was why she loved him, most likely. She'd have fallen for anyone who happened along, probably. He was nothing special, just a man. Just a hurt man she had helped. That didn't mean she owned him.

She was a stupid woman to cry over a man who was really a stranger. And she would never do it again; she swore it to herself. Two more tears squeezed from between her tight-closed eyes and leaked over her cheeks toward her ears as she lay on her back. Serve her right to cry into her own ears.

The really stupid part was her thinking that he could love her back. She had forgotten about her hair for the moment, forgotten that she was bald as a baby all over. Likely he had already noticed she had no eyebrows, no hair on her arms. How could a man love a freak like her? She had to remember life had dealt her a bad hand, but it was the only hand she had and she had to play it out. Being a freak was tough, but not nearly so tough when you *knew* you were a freak and expected nothing because that was what you were likely to get.

She listened to his steady breathing as she let her eyes leak all they wanted. Sometimes a woman just needed to cry, even a freak woman. Life could be so hard.

Wiley lay there on the hard floor and listened to her go to bed. She blew out the light, lay back, and never moved again; she was probably asleep at once. She was likely bone weary all the way through and it was his fault. Tending a sick man was hard on a body, especially a little woman like her. That must be it. She was just plain wore out. No wonder she wanted him gone.

She was a special little thing, full of fire and guts like a she bear, only she must be getting near her limits. Imagine settling here just 'cause it was where her folks were buried. Imagine being out here all alone for years. And such a pretty thing too. His angel. 'Course, he'd never call her that—made him blush just to think of saying it out loud. But she would always be that nebulous creature he first saw, floating over him when he tried to focus his eyes, that wondrous, beautiful creature who looked not of this world. He knew he would be able to close his eyes and see her that way for the rest of his life, whenever he wanted.

And she was lying over there sound asleep in the same bed he had occupied for so many days. Just over there, barely out of reach, and yet she might as well be a real angel for all the chance he stood of knowing her any better. His angel was also a woman, and he must be getting better for sure if he could think of her in that way.

He owed her his life. That was all there was to it. He would be dead on the prairie without her, so he owed her everything. And she wanted him gone. Best he could do for her was to do like she wanted and get out as soon as he could. That's what she wanted. That was all he could do for her.

But for now, for right now, he was so tired all the time. He drifted into the warmth of sleep. The last thing he heard was her soft breathing—just over there.

''Yeah, he was here,'' said the bartender. ''Had one drink, bought three bottles of whiskey, and left. Wasn't here more'n five minutes all together.''

Steve sighed and considered his options.

He could go after Davey, but that would likely take days to find him. He could have gone in most any direction. Even if Steve *did* find him, likely the money would be gone. If it did take days, the ranch really wouldn't wait very well. Too many things needed doing out there.

And then there was Alfred. The boy shouldn't be left all alone like that. He was almost a man, sure enough, but to suddenly drop the load of the ranch and chores on his shoulders was too much to ask. Nothing to it but to head on out to the place, get to work, and figure that maybe someday Davey would dry out and come back home if he wasn't too ashamed.

What really bothered Steve was Dave's attitude when he had been drinking. Some men grew friendly as whiskey took them in. Some men grew almighty affectionate to women. Davey, though,

Davey got just plain mean. That's why he had been in prison in the first place.

Steve pushed out the swinging doors and stepped out on the boardwalk. Things looked peaceful and quiet in town, only he knew that things were not really that peaceful and quiet anywhere. Everybody had troubles. The few people he saw, sweeping in front of their stores or coming and going, all had troubles, likely just as serious as his.

For some reason, the new teacher popped into his mind. Now there was a girl you wouldn't think would have any troubles to look at her. Only she did. Her paw had been killed, she had that sick man she was tending, and she had a job to pay mind to. She had her troubles, sure enough. She stood them well, though. She could still smile and be friendly and worry about her troubles herownself. That was a good trait in a woman—a good trait in most anybody.

He walked out to where Lopez was ground-tied and swung aboard. Might as well get on back to the ranch. There was work to be done, twice as much as before.

Lopez's hooves clip-clopped down the dusty street. Front Street. How come every western town Steve had ever been in had a street called Front Street?

The schoolhouse was the last building on the street, and just before Steve got there, the door opened and the kids came out for morning recess. Some headed around the rear while the others scattered around the yard playing like the kids they were. It was a good thing for kids to play while they could. Once grown up, life didn't allow much time for playing and having fun.

A few of the older ones already beyond the playing age were standing around in a small group talking. Alfred was on the outside of the group just listening.

The teacher, Katherine, came out and watched the children for a moment, then looked up and caught his eye as he was ready to ride past. On impulse he reined in by the gate. Katherine studied him for a moment then walked over.

"Hello, Mr. Skobrak," she said.

"Name's Steve, ma'am." She nodded.

"And mine is Katie," she said, "but I think it would be best to keep on a formal level, at least while the children are about."

He nodded and swung down. Didn't seem right to be looking down on her from a tall horse. Even from the ground, she didn't hardly come up more than his shoulders.

"How is your first day going?" he asked.

"Going just fine, thank you." Of course she couldn't really say anything else, only it was going real fine. The kids were respectful and well behaved. Probably each and every one of them had been threatened by their parents. Only Simon was a little unusual. He kept looking at her with a strange intensity, a look that made her just a little uncomfortable sometimes.

She looked up at Steve, looking him straight in the eye. He took off his hat and began to twist it in his hands unconsciously. His hair was tousled.

"Alfred been behaving?" he asked.

"A perfect gentleman," she said.

Simon came flying backward from the group of older kids and landed on his back in the grass. Alfred came and stood over him, fists clenched, jaw set hard.

"I stand corrected," said Katie, then turned and

went over to the two boys, now in the center of a circle of kids. Simon leaped to his feet, ready to go after his assailant.

"Stop!" Katie said, and he stopped at once. Alfred stood there, casual but ready. Steve recognized the look. Apparently Alfred had decided that something was worth fighting about, and once that decision was made, he was prepared to carry it out to the conclusion. That kid had a streak in him that sometimes made Steve uncomfortable about hisownself. Blood was for sure thicker than water and he could sometimes see a lot of himself in Alfred.

Katie took each of the boys by the arm, and none too gently.

"I do not care what the fight was about," she said. "You will both go home for the rest of the day. When you show up tomorrow you will have written 'I will not fight at school' five hundred times. You will also have a note from your parents or bring your parents with you. Is that clear?"

"Yes'm," said Alfred. He looked over at his uncle, and Katie could clearly see the shame in Alfred's eyes. Alfred obviously thought a lot of his uncle.

Simon turned and stalked away, saying nothing. Katie watched him leave walking straight and tall. He had been shamed twice, once by Alfred, who dumped him so unceremoniously in the grass, and once by the teacher chastising him in front of the others—and him almost a man. Katie wondered if she had been too strict.

Alfred turned to go, then turned back.

"Ma'am?"

"Yes, Alfred." He looked at his feet, obviously ashamed.

"I . . . uhh . . . cannot write, ma'am."

Katie thought it over.

"In that case, I want you to write out your ABCs," she said. "Do it ten times. Your uncle or father will show you how."

"Yes'm," he said, and turned to go.

"Alfred?" He stopped, back to her.

"Ma'am?"

"Why did you hit him?"

"Rather not say, ma'am."

Katie wondered what Simon had said that prompted such a violent reaction. Maybe violence ran in the family. She looked over at Steve. He was watching, face expressionless. Katie wondered what he was thinking.

"What did he say?" Steve asked as Alfred walked his horse beside him. No heat, no anger, just curiosity. Boy must've had a reason. Alfred thought about his answer while they rode in silence, clip-clopping down Front Street into town. Behind, the sound of kids faded as they went back into the school.

"Man hadn't ought to talk about a woman that way, least not a good woman," Alfred finally said. Steve nodded. He had figured as much.

"About the teacher, huh?" he asked.

"Yup."

They pulled up in front of the store and swung down. For the first time, Alfred seemed to notice where they were.

"What we doin' here?" he asked.

"Got to get you some paper and a book with the ABCs," Steve said. "You heard what she said you had to do."

"Can I get some candy?" Sometimes Alfred forgot he was supposed to be acting like a man.

Sometimes he slipped and acted the part of a fourteen-year-old—Not often, but sometimes.

"We'll see," Steve said. "Depends on how much a book and some paper costs."

"*McGuffey's Primer* here is ten cents," said Mayor Hanson. "First thing in it is the ABCs. Can of peaches is twenty cents and the paper is another dime. That comes to forty cents."

"I'll be havin' some of that licorice too," Steve said.

Cyrus took some out of the jar and laid it on top of the other stuff.

"Forty-one cents," he said. Steve put a silver dollar on the counter and Cyrus handed him the change.

"Don't need any ink or pens, do you?" Cyrus asked.

"Nope. Got 'em at the ranch." The door opened and a real hefty woman came in. Cyrus turned to her, and in no time the two people, one man and one almost man, were riding toward the ranch once more. Alfred turned his head and watched the school as they rode past, then they were out of town and on the way home. They rode in silence for fifteen minutes.

"Ain't no nice way to tell you this," Steve said finally. Alfred looked over at him expectantly.

"Davey's gone," Steve said. Alfred's expression did not change.

"Figured he would go pretty soon," Alfred said. The horses clopped toward the ranch. Finally he asked, "He take the money, did he?"

"Yup."

"Likely he won't be back," Alfred said.

"Likely not."

"Good." And after a minute, Alfred booted his horse into a canter. Steve held back and let him go, figuring the boy maybe needed to be alone a little. The kid had taken it real good, like a man.

Chapter Nine

"Oh, Lord," Walter moaned as he twisted in the bed, trying to get away from the never-ending agony in his belly. It was as if some small animal was chewing at him in there, gnawing pieces from his innards, then pouring acid on the open wounds. Just as bad, his hands and feet felt as if someone was holding them in a fire, and the skin was frying and cracking and peeling away from the moist tissue underneath. It was all he could do to keep from screaming. He could see Katie watching him from where she sat at the kitchen table.

"Laudanum, Katie," he said—no, moaned, actually.

"I hate to give you any more, Walter," she said. He could feel a wave of fear. He had to have the laudanum and the ultimate fuzzy relief the harsh-tasting stuff brought. It was the only way to make the sharp hard hurt ease back some, the only way to make life even a little bit bearable.

"I got to have it," he said. "I cannot wait another minute." Sweat beaded on his forehead. Inside his bowels rumbled and moved, twisting snakes of hot fire inside him low down in his belly. He groaned again. "Oh, Lord!" he said. Katie sighed and came over.

"I guess it will make you sleep easier," she said and reached for the bottle, that glorious bottle, on the shelf over his head. He could easily see the shelf and the bottle, that brown glass container that held the blessed relief, only it might as well be in another town as far as he was concerned. He was far too weak to reach it.

He had tried. He had tried while she was in school today—and yesterday. Likely he would try while she was in school tomorrow. Only the darned thing was too far up, too far by inches, and he lay there all day, twisting away from the awful pain in his insides and counting the slow ticks of the clock on the wall. He counted each long pain-filled second, each minute, each hour until she would be home and he could have another dose of wondrous, rotten-tasting relief.

Katie held the big spoon to his trembling lips and watched as he eagerly sucked at the liquid. Sometimes she got tired of his endless grunting and moaning from the pain—any human would—and this was one of those times. She had planning to do for her class tomorrow, and his endless whimpering was distracting. Besides, a good night's sleep might help him regain a little of his lost strength. She gave him an extra spoonful of the stuff, and he sucked greedily on the spoon, determined to get every last drop of relief he could.

"Thank you," he said. "Thank you, thank you." He laid back on the twisted blankets and waited for the fuzziness to come over him and blanket the pain.

"You're welcome, Walter," she said. She sat there on the bed beside him, looking down on the suffering man. Katie could actually see the laudanum going to work on him as the frantic expression in his eyes eased. The twisted skin of his forehead relaxed as the medicine took him in, and for the first time that day he relaxed, breathing a long but normal sigh, not one that was forced through tense, screaming muscles.

Walter looked so tired from his daily battle with the awful pain in his innards. It was amazing that he continued to fight against the pain. It seemed he should have given in to it long ago and let himself die. Come to think of it, he was looking awfully weak, worse than ever. Maybe now was the time.

But it usually didn't work that way, least not up to now. He would get to his weakest, then start to get better. The pain would ease and he would get to relax and sleep more, and then he would be rested and feeling better. Katie could see in his eyes when Walter would begin to hope the worst of it was over, when he would think the sickness was gone and life would flow back into his body. The look of hope would appear, the look of cautious optimism. Then, as time went on, the hope would be replaced with something else, a look of certainty. He *was* better. The pain was almost completely gone. He knew he would recover his lost strength and his life would go on.

Then, when he was certain he was getting well, when he was feeling his best, when he was concerned mainly with healing and regaining his strength, when he started being less and less cautious about what kinds of food he was eating, the pain would return as savage and unbearable as before. The look of despair in his eyes when that happened was almost indescribable; the disappointment, the fear in there was so overpowering as to be almost worse than the pain itself.

This weekly cycle had occurred three times so far, and the doctor was powerless to do anything except provide laudanum. Katie was relegated to supporting the miserable, suffering man in any way she could. There was not much she could do really except watch him slowly dwindle away in agony and give him laudanum when he could stand the pain no longer and had suffered all and more than a man could stand.

Walter couldn't understand why she withheld the laudanum, why she didn't keep him submerged in the soft fuzzy netherworld the stuff brought on, but he trusted her and knew she would not make him suffer needlessly. Likely something bad would happen if he took too much of the stuff. Besides, he couldn't reach the bottle himself. Probably just as well. Likely he would drink it down, drink the nasty stuff in long swallows that would bring on the soft easing of the pain so heavy he would be carried away into the softness, and no matter how bad the pain was, Walter wasn't ready to die. Not yet. They might be waiting for him.

In the clouds of laudanum he sometimes saw them, the men he had killed. He could see them standing there as if they were waiting for him. They'd be standing there, oblivious to their awful wounds and their own slippery blood, just waiting for him.

Sometimes they would reach out slimy blood-covered hands toward him, ready to take him in and do god-knows-what to him. And he was afraid. He would swim to the top of his fuzzy comfort, swim back toward the red of the awful pain just so he would know he was still alive and they could not get him yet.

He knew what they wanted. They wanted him to

tell, to explain to the living what had happened to them, how they had been snatched from the living and forced into death by him. That's what they wanted. They wanted their kin to know where they were and why—and who had done it.

But he couldn't tell their kin, on account of he didn't know their names. They were just men, anonymous men he had killed from ambush, and he didn't know enough about them to tell their kin from anybody else. So he couldn't do what they wanted. And they were waiting for him.

'Course, he did know about Katie's father. He could tell her, and maybe at least one of those specters would vanish into the mist. And he would tell too, but only when he knew for sure he was dying. When the darkness settled in on him, he would tell her. Just before he died. Maybe then her father would leave that awful group. Maybe that would be one less for him to deal with.

The laudanum gradually swept him up and carried him along in the soft, billowy clouds. The real world eased back, faded into the surreal swells of soft and warm and fuzzy.

Katie looked down on the sleeping man and sighed. She was tired, tired clear through. Caring for a sick man with no hope of survival was hard on a body, even a young body like her. She was hungry too, but somehow couldn't force herself to face the cooking stove. Tonight she would eat at the café. It would be nice to see Alice again, anyway. She rose to her feet and began to fix her hair.

Marcus lay abed, trying to ignore the numerous fall flies buzzing around the room. For the entire first week after his leg had been near shot off, he spent most of his waking moments trying to keep them from lighting on his awful wounded knee, and because of their mindless persistence he had developed a hatred for the insects that burned intense and undying.

He wanted to catch them, each and every one. And then he wanted to kill them slowly, lingering over the deaths, taking nourishment from their suffering.

Once in a while he would actually get one, catching the buzzing tormentor in one of his wildly waving hands. He would disable the nasty thing, pulling off wings and legs slowly, one at a time, and watching the results. It was one of his bigger disappointments that the darned things could not scream.

He had no illusions about his condition. He would survive, but he would be a stiff-legged cripple, the wounded leg shorter than the other now that there was no knee to speak of. He would stutter-step along, an object of scorn and pity for the rest of his life and no self-respecting woman would want anything to do with him. It was all that cowboy's fault. Him and that woman who screamed. Hadn't been for those two, his life would be going on as normal instead of the way it was.

His hatred for them was just as bad as for the flies. Sometimes he toyed with the idea of killing them the same way as the flies, taking them off a piece at a time and watching them squirm. Only thing is, they *would* scream.

Sometimes he would lie there, flapping his hands frantically at the buzzing bluebottles, but in his mind he would be somewhere else. He would be with the cowboy or with the woman, and they would be mighty unhappy.

He would torment the helpless cowboy in his mind, taking hours of pleasure at the man's agony, and in the end he would not kill the man, but rather leave him tied and helpless to die slowly of thirst and hunger, leave him with clouds of flies buzzing around *his* open wounds.

But the woman, now she had something special in store for her. The hours Marcus spent with her would be horror of a different kind. But in the end, she too would be left helpless and crying. She would be left alone to face the slowest, most horrible death he could imagine.

His life would not improve just because they were dead, Marcus knew that. But when his leg would be hurting, or kids would be pointing and laughing, he would be able to take out the memories of those two in their dying agony and bathe himself in them. They wouldn't make him whole again, but they might ease his angry mind, make the humiliation and pain easier to bear.

He looked down the length of the filthy bed, past the shiny huge scab that had hardened over what had been his knee, and out the dirty window. Far down the street, he saw the cowboy herding a steer into town. He was too far away to recognize his face, but Marcus didn't need to see his face. Marcus had memorized everything about that man, the way he walked, the way he stood, the way he wore his hat. That was the cowboy, all right, and Marcus let his hate flow out the window, wishing he could strike the man down from where he lay.

But he couldn't, and the man pushed the steer down Front Street and around back of the café. Likely Old Man Carley would butcher the thing tomorrow and pretty Alice would be serving fresh steak by nightfall. Pretty Alice had always been a little cold to him, but now that he was a cripple she would for sure not have anything to do with him.

Marcus lay there, flies almost forgotten as he waited for the man to reappear. In a few minutes, he came out the door and crossed the street to the general store. He was probably paying some on his account, maybe picking up some supplies.

Paying some on account was another thought that bothered Marcus. His money, once so easy to come by in the gambling games, was almost gone. This miserable shack, foul-smelling and filthy as it was, would be coldly and harshly denied to him if his money ran out. Mr. Tanker was not one to give credit to anyone, least of all a gambling man.

Two weeks left. That was all. Then his rent would be done and he would have to get out or pay another ten dollars to the old skinflint. It might be he could walk, or sort of walk, by that time. To save ten whole dollars he could camp out on the prairie and put up with the hated outdoors. He had his thoughts of vengeance to keep him warm.

He snapped to attention as the woman came out from beside the saloon and walked across the street to the café. He was focused on her so hard he didn't notice the cowboy come out of the store and stop, also watching the woman cross the street. The woman went inside the café, and Marcus's eyes popped over to the cowboy as he also crossed the street and went into the café.

Marcus lay back on the bed, tired from his exertion. He thought it was funny the two of them going in the same place like that. Maybe the cowboy was moving on the woman. Likely she wouldn't be interested, but a body never could tell about women. If the two of them *were* interested in each other, that might present a whole bunch of new ideas for his getting even, lots of new ideas. He let himself drift back into his mind, back to someplace where he was in control and let his head play with the idea. He didn't know it, but he was smiling. It had been a long time since he had smiled.

She was sitting at the table in the corner by herself, and she had that aura of special aloneness that a woman showed when she was eating alone. Most women never did eat out by themselves. It was as if eating alone in public cast a doubt on their ability to catch a man to take care of them, as if she was an object deserving of pity. A woman eating alone in public was a mighty rare thing to find.

Banker Short and his wife were the only other ones in there, although a table full of dirty dishes testified to the memory of other diners this day.

Short looked up at Steve and nodded. Of all the people in the world, Short probably knew more about Steve and his financial situation than anybody. He held the mortgage on the ranch. He had heard about Steve's brother running out and knew about the kid now in Steve's care (although the boy was more than a kid for sure).

When he first heard about the brother's flight, Banker Short had been worried. The ranch didn't represent a whole lot of money, but he didn't want to own another ranch. He already owned three and was having trouble getting any buyers. Ranching was hard, never-ending work, and most folks seemed more anxious to take jobs in town if they could find them. 'Course, the Indians might have had something to do with it too, even though they had been well behaved of late.

Then Steve had come in and sat down and told it to Short just like it was. He had been uncomfortable telling another man about his family, but he hadn't held back anything. He had explained about his brother's fondness for the bottle and his propensity toward violence when imbibing. He had said how he would run the ranch himself, him and the boy, and gave his word that Short would get his money and would not be sorry that he had loaned it in the first place. Banker Short had believed him. A man of honor was worth a little trust.

"I'll just keep figuring the interest," he had heard himself say. "If you can keep that up to date, why, you can pay on the principal whenever you can." And Steve had shook his hand and thanked him; it was something that didn't bear thinking on anymore because they both knew it would be taken care of.

For an instant Banker Short couldn't figure what Steve was doing in the café on account of it wasn't like him to squander his money on bought food. Then Short saw him glance over at the new teacher. Oh, that was it! Short allowed the corners of his mouth to turn up in a knowing smile as he turned back to his own dinner and his wife, who was still not talking to him.

Steve walked over to her table and Katie looked up at him with an expression he could not fathom at all.

"Howdy, Miss Withrow," Steve said and took off his hat.

"Good evening, Mr. Skobrak." There was no note of interest in her voice, but no note of dismissal either. It was just the tone of a teacher meeting up with the guardian of one of her pupils.

"You fixing to eat alone?" he asked, amazed at his brashness. Mostly his mouth didn't say things without him thinking them over first.

"Why, yes," she said. "Are you?"

"Uhh, yes, ma'am," he said. Actually, the

thought hadn't entered his mind. The idea of paying cash money for a meal didn't set real good with him, not while he was owing another man money, anyway.

"Why don't you sit down here," she said. "I'd be pleased to have the company." She suddenly flushed as she realized what she had said. That was pretty brazen for a woman: in fact, it was more than brazen, it was almost hussylike. What must he be thinking of her?

"Why, thank you, Miss Withrow," he said. And then he was sitting there opposite her, a big man with broad shoulders and weathered face, and she remembered him shooting that other man in the knee just like it was yesterday. She didn't know what to say, and the silence stretched out for a minute.

Alice had been on the way out from the kitchen when Steve had come through the door, and curiosity had made her stop in the doorway and wait to see what he was back here for. He hadn't left but maybe ten minutes ago. Being a woman, it didn't take her too long to figure why he was here, and she smiled as she watched the two of them fumble around trying to figure a decent way to sit together. She happened to catch Banker Short's eye, and the two of them smiled like conspirators as they listened to Steve and Katie awkwardly and finally get the job done. Once Steve was planted across from Katie, Alice came on out.

"Evening," she said. "What'll it be tonight? Got some roast beef left if you're in a hurry."

"That'll be fine," Katie said, trying to read what Alice was thinking. She probably thought Katie was a nasty, evil woman to be sitting there breaking bread with a man she hardly knew. Maybe Alice thought even worse, and she felt herself flush again.

Steve saw the color come up in her face again and wondered briefly why women flushed red like that for no real reason at all. It couldn't be on account of him, that was for sure, unless she was embarrassed some to be seen with him in such a public place.

"Beef sounds good to me," he said, and wondered what he was going to say to Katie once Alice went back to the kitchen.

"Food'll be up real soon," Alice said. "I'll fetch you some coffee while you are waiting."

Katie hated coffee, but for some reason said nothing. Alice headed back into the kitchen and they were alone together, sort of. Steve cleared his throat.

"So how's Alfred doing?" he asked.

"Your nephew is progressing rapidly," Katie said. "He is determined to master reading, and I expect he is working diligently in the evenings."

"Yup," said Steve. "He works some every night before bed. He practices his letters."

"That's good." Silence. Now what? What could you say to a stranger of the opposite sex. What could you say to a man who popped into a body's mind at the strangest times? What could you say to a man who could shoot into another man with absolutely no display of emotion whatsoever?

"Has he been in any more trouble with that other boy?" Steve finally asked. It seemed the only thing they had to talk about was Alfred. He was a fool for having come in here in the first place. But she was so darned pretty. . . .

"No," she said. Actually, the two young men had stayed clear of each other. Simon still looked at her with that strange intensity, as if he knew something about her that nobody else knew, but he had never done anything bad she could put her finger on. Alfred always seemed to be around though, at least whenever it seemed as if she and Simon would be alone together. In a way she was glad. She did not want to be alone with Simon. He was almost a man, and she remembered the scribbling of the last teacher, writing his name over and over again. It might be best if Simon was not alone with her.

She sipped at her coffee, recoiled from the bitter taste. She couldn't even remember Alice setting it down in front of her. It didn't taste any better than it ever had. It always amazed her how something that smelled so good could taste so bad.

"Don't care for it, huh?" Steve asked. Apparently she had wrinkled up her nose. She smiled rather sheepishly.

"To tell the truth, I have never cared for coffee," she confessed.

"How come you took some?"

"I guess you make me a little nervous, Mr. Skobrak," she said. He grinned.

"That's okay, Miss Withrow," he said. "You make me a whole lot nervous too."

She laughed a little-girl laugh. He surprised her with his openness.

"I am not used to eating supper with strange men," she said. "Especially men who are so handy with a pistol."

He frowned a little.

"I am not a gunman, Miss Withrow," he said earnestly. "I am just a rancher." There was a short pause. "A gun is just a tool."

"So tell me a little about your ranch, Mr. Skobrak,'' she said. She thought it better to get the conversation away from that deadly blue-steel gun.

''You can just call me Steve if you want,'' he said. ''No need to be so polite and formal all the time.''

Katie thought about that for a moment, then decided she didn't want to be so formal and polite with him all the time. She knew it would be looked on wrong by the town, but at the moment she didn't seem to care much.

''Okay, Steve,'' she said. ''And when we are away from the school, you may call me Katie.''

''Katie or Katherine?'' he asked.

''Your choice,'' she said.

''Then I choose Katherine,'' he said. ''Sounds real nice. Sort of rolls off the tongue. Almost like poetry.'' He suddenly realized how silly that sounded and felt himself grow red under his tan. For gosh sakes, he was acting just like a schoolboy.

Alice wiped the grin from her face and carried out the supper. If they only knew how easy it was to hear every word they said, they'd for sure be a little more careful about each and every word. She could see Banker Short smiling at his table, and his wife was smiling too, which was quite an improvement over her mood when she had first come in.

Short and his wife got up and left while Alice was setting stuff on the table, and then Alice went back to the kitchen and they were alone, really alone, for the first time ever.

''So tell me about your ranch,'' Katie said. ''I have never been on a ranch.''

''Ranching is a different way of life,'' Steve began, ''but at least a man is on his own and can make of it what he will.''

And that was how the conversation started. They

talked about his ranch and about her teaching for the first time. They talked about Alfred and how he was making out, and about the sick man she was tending in her home. Before long they were like old friends, catching up on things that had happened since the last time they had met. But they weren't old friends, and later on when they were all alone, they would suddenly realize that something special had happened and their lives had been changed forever.

Alice stood just inside the kitchen door, listening to every word. She knew it was wrong to listen, but not much happened in a small town, and even if it was wrong, she wanted to hear and that was that. Not that she would blab it all over town. She wasn't that type of person. She just thought it was awfully romantic. And it was.

Chapter Ten

Virginia had to jump on the shovel to get it into the ground. Not that the ground was so dry and hard, just that she didn't weigh very much. It would take three or four two-footed jumps to get the blade to slide far enough so she could pry up the soil and display the potatoes that had been growing hidden from her eyes. Even though she had planted them herself, it was always a surprise that they were really under there, all those round and oblong dirt-covered balls. She always planted quite a few because they kept so well over the winter, but the harvesting was backbreaking work for one of such diminutive stature.

She knelt and picked out the potatoes, smelling the earthy smell of fresh-turned soil as she did so. Off in the distance, way off in the distance, thunder mumbled over the horizon in a promise of rain to come, probably after dark. It would be easier digging tomorrow, most likely.

She picked out eight potatoes, eight more guarantees against the pains of hunger throughout the long winter season, and placed them carefully on the piece of canvas she used to transport her harvest from the field to the small, underground pit she used for winter food storage. When she harvested the row of potato hills farther away from the house, she would bring the wagon, but for now it seemed just as fast to carry them back by hand.

She took the shovel and moved back a step to widen the turned earth, to make certain she missed not even one of the precious things. Then she began her long-practiced hop up and down on the shovel. She was already breathing hard as she jumped and stomped the tool into the ground and that was why she never heard the two of them coming. Suddenly they were just there—two men, one young, one not so young—sitting high on their horses looking down on the hard-working woman.

''Howdy, mister,'' said one, and Virginia jerked in surprise and spun to face them. Her hands went for her head automatically, but it was all right, her bandanna was still firmly in place.

Mister, the man had called her, likely because of her bulky, oversize clothes. It wouldn't hurt to have them think she was a man. She nodded at them but said nothing.

''We could use some water,'' said the other. They both dressed like cowhands, what with their spurs and chaps and such.

Virginia nodded toward the creek. ''Water's free,'' she said in as deep a voice as she could muster. The first one, the older one, looked at her hard for a minute.

''Didn't know there was anybody out here,'' he said. Virginia thought he was making talk, trying to get her to speak again. She shrugged in reply.

''Potatoes look right plentiful this year,'' he said. For men who were thirsty they did not seem in a real hurry to get down to the water. She nodded.

''Might be we could buy some off'n you?'' he asked. Virginia was suddenly interested. Here was maybe an opportunity to make a little money. She could always use a little money.

''How many you want?'' she asked in her low, manlike voice. At least she hoped it was a manlike voice. He touched his horse with his spurs and suddenly she was trapped between the two horses.

''Well, I'll be,'' he said as he looked down on her. ''This here's a woman, I do declare.''

His friend laughed a silly, little-boy giggle. ''She don't look like no woman I ever seen,'' he said.

''It's all them clothes she has on,'' said the first. Virginia could smell the sour smell of whiskey on his breath. His eyes were red, kind of watery, and looked sore.

''She is dressed like a man sure enough,'' he said. He kept her between the two horses as she looked about, trying to figure how to get back to the house and her gun. All of a sudden she figured she would mighty like to have her big gun handy. The shovel was there, but it was stuck in the ground good and solid. Likely she wouldn't get a chance to use it as a weapon even if she did get it out of the ground. She wasn't sure why she thought she might need a weapon.

''Where's your man?'' asked the older one as he looked around.

''He should be back from town anytime now,'' she said. ''He went to get his rifle fixed because it was shooting a little high.''

The man laughed.

''Now how come I do not believe you? How come I don't think you would be out here digging potatoes all alone if you really had a man around here? Ain't no ring on your finger, neither,'' he observed.

These two weren't bad men, she thought. It was more like they were just a little bit drunk and maybe a bit curious. Paw used to get to drinking once in a while, and he had never done anything bad. Likely these two had just stopped for water and would ride on. Most men wouldn't rob or hurt or do anything bad to a woman out here. Women were too scarce.

''The water is over there in the creek,'' she said and tried to walk around the horse to get to her shovel. But the horse stayed right there.

''You want to move so I can get back to work?'' she asked. He looked down on her for a long moment as if he was seeing her for the first time, as if she had just come into focus in his bleary eyes.

''Sorry,'' he said, and suddenly the horse was no longer hemming her in. The two of them rode down to the creek where they dismounted under the trees. Virginia breathed a sigh of relief. For a minute there, she hadn't known what to expect or what was going to happen, and she hated that feeling of helplessness, really hated it.

But the two were likely just cowhands out working, or maybe having just been let go on account of winter coming up shortly. It must be a hard, lonely way of life, being a cowhand. Of course, they at least each had a friend. She didn't even have a friend at all, except for Wiley, and he wasn't exactly a friend.

She pried up on the shovel and the earth bulged and split open as she pushed the handle down. Lots of potatoes showed in the dirt and she bent over and began to pull them loose, keeping her eye on the two men.

They watered up pretty good, talking heatedly,

although she couldn't hear what they were saying. Virginia picked up her canvas of potatoes and toted it toward the house, trying to look casual as she lugged the heavy thing. The weight pulled her over to one side and she sort of wobbled as she walked. It really was time to go to the house anyway, for the load was about all she could handle. Besides, probably be a fair idea to go get her big pistol. Just in case.

But she didn't make it but halfway, and then that horse was right in front of her again, between her and the house. She sighed and set the heavy potatoes down. Now what?

"You wouldn't be looking to hire on a couple of good men, would you?" asked the man. "Probably be right handy for a lone woman to have two good men around to help out for the winter." The tone of his voice said that his meaning was not necessarily what was in his words.

Virginia did not like this whole situation. Mother had told her it was not a good idea for a woman to be alone with men although she'd never really told her why exactly, and she was almighty alone out here. Suddenly these men did not seem near so friendly and Virginia wanted them to be gone, wanted things to change back to normal.

"Sorry," she said. "Cannot afford to hire anybody. Don't even have any money for myself." She made to pick up the canvas again, but the horse pushed her back.

"David," said the younger man, the one who was watching from a little piece away. "Let's get on out of here," he added. David ignored him, kept pushing her back with his horse.

"What're you doing?" she asked angrily. "Stop

pushing that horse into me.'' He laughed a strange little laugh.

''Got something else I'd like to push into you,'' he said.

Virginia had no idea what he was talking about, but she was getting angry.

''Get that horse away from me!'' she said loud and harsh. David just laughed.

''David!'' said his friend, voice hard. ''This ain't right. Let us go.''

''Don't fret none, Peter,'' David said. ''She is all alone out here, and I ain't even *seen* a woman for two months.''

''This ain't right,'' Peter said. ''Let's go to town if'n you must, but this ain't right at all.''

David swung down and was suddenly standing there right in front of her, blocking her escape to the house. He was so much bigger than she was. Virginia was suddenly afraid but she wasn't sure why. What did he want? What was he going to do?

She had her answer quick enough, as he reached out and suddenly had her wrapped in his arms. He pulled her to him, and for the first time in her life, she felt the hard body of a man pressed up against hers. For an instant she was so shocked she didn't know what to do, then she began to struggle against his arms, trying to break away. But he was young and strong, ever so strong. She could smell his smell of stale sweat, dirty clothes, and old whiskey, and hear him breathing wetly down into her ear.

''David!'' said Peter. ''I am leaving.'' Like a threat almost.

''Sure, Peter,'' David said loud as can be, almost directly into her ear. ''You go on ahead if'n you've a mind to, and I'll be along shortly.''

''What you're doing ain't right,'' Peter said, and

for a moment Virginia had a little hope. Maybe Peter would stop him. Then she felt despair wash through her as she heard Peter's horse ride away—fast. And then she was alone with David, held fast in his arms, trying not to pay too much mind to his bad smell.

''Quit your wigglin',' ' he said wetly into her ear. ''You're gonna' like this just fine, I'm thinkin'.'' Virginia obviously wasn't getting anywhere with all her struggling, so she relaxed and waited to see what was coming next.

'' 'At's better,'' he said. Virginia was thinking that it sure felt weird to be held on to by another person, when suddenly she was on the ground on her back and he was sort of on top of her holding her down with his weight. She could smell the freshly dug earth from the potato hill by her head, and feel the softness of the loosened soil underneath her.

It was then she suddenly realized that the worst thing that could have happened to her had just happened. Her bandanna had slipped from her head. He could see her bare naked head! She squirmed like crazy, wanting desperately to get her arms loose so she could put her bandanna back where it belonged, but she was helpless under his weight.

''What the . . . ?'' she heard him say in surprise, and he pulled his upper body back and looked down at her bald head.

''How come you did that?'' he asked, awful breath coming down over her like a wavering cloud. She felt herself flush, and squirmed with all her strength to get her hands loose. She had never been so confused, so helpless, so embarrassed all at once in her whole life. But she could not move and finally had to give up the struggle and lie there panting under his weight while he studied her bald head.

"Ain't never seen no bald woman before," he said, almost to himself. Virginia closed her eyes in her humiliation.

"Guess it don't matter none," David finally said. "Least it don't make no difference where it counts." She looked up at him. He had a really strange smile, as if his teeth were gritted together.

"Now you just lay still," he said through that weird smile. "This won't take hardly no time at all."

Virginia was concentrating on his face, on his rheumy eyes really, and it was a surprise to see the front end of a Colt come into view slowly and stick against his ear. The ratcheting click of a hammer being slowly cocked sounded awful loud to her, but it must have sounded like the cracking of doom stuck in his ear like that. David became absolutely, rock-solid still, as if he was made of stone. His eyes opened wide and stayed that way. The liquor wasn't bothering him anymore.

"You want to close your eyes a minute, Virginia?" Wiley asked, voice real quiet. David Skobrak whined softly. He figured he was dead.

Katie folded another sheet of paper into four sections as Simon's voice droned on in the background, struggling with the lovely flowery language of the Bible. She quickly stitched up one side of the fold, took up her scissors and cut across the top, making in effect a small book of four pages. She then wrote "The Cat Ate the Bat" in her normal flowing handwriting across the top of the first page.

This would be Alfred's next copybook, and it would be his job to copy what she had written until the first page was full. Each day she would write something a little more advanced for each of the children. Each day they would fill the page. Simon droned on and it was the typical beginning of another school day.

Only it didn't seem like just another typical day. Her mind kept taking her back to the previous evening, taking her back to the time in the café with Steve.

The meal had been over so fast she couldn't believe it; the time had been sucked away without their knowing while they talked, although she couldn't really remember exactly what they had said or talked about. She could remember his face, especially his eyes, and she could remember every nuance of every expression, could actually see him in her mind, clear and smiling and friendly.

It had felt as if everybody in town had been watching them—watching her watching him was more like the truth—only she hadn't cared at all. Rather, she had been proud to be with him, to be seen with him, and she didn't understand in the bright light of morning exactly what she had been feeling and thinking in the purple dusk of last night. She did understand that it had been important to her, a changing in her, so to speak.

And she knew she wanted to see him again. She wanted to see and be seen with this cold hard shooter of men who didn't seem nearly so cold and hard anymore. Suddenly she was aware that Simon had stopped reading and the entire class was staring at her.

"You want I should read more, ma'am?" he asked. His eyes traveled up and down her body like slime from a swamp, and she thought about how young he was, even though he was but a year or two younger than she was at most.

"That'll be all, Simon," she said and began to hand out the new copybooks. When she got to Alfred, he looked up at her and something in his eyes reminded her of Steve. She handed him the book and moved on, annoyed by the nagging return into her mind of that disturbing man.

Eight miles away, Steve pounded home the staple and straightened from his work on the fence. The wire stretched back to the corner of the corral, maybe a dozen fence posts away. He took off his hat and wiped the sweat from his brow with his forearm, then planted the hat back where it belonged.

Something looked a little strange back there, and he looked harder at the top strand of wire. Sure enough, two posts back it was hanging loose. He must not have stapled it there. He shook his head in disgust and walked back. Now what could a man be thinking of that he would forget what he was doing?

"So they had dinner together last night, huh?" asked the mayor. Alice looked up from the bolt of material she was examining.

"Sure did," she said. "Seemed to get along real fine too." She smiled as she remembered, then returned to examining the cloth. It was real silk, not what a working girl like her needed, but it sure was pretty.

"You know anything about him?" she asked casually. Mayor Hanson was busy wiping some flour from the counter where Elizabeth Right had spilled it before she left.

"Skobrak seems like a good man far as I know," he said, shaking his dusting cloth on the floor.

"Brother doesn't seem like too much, though. Heard he took all their money and pulled out."

Alice looked up, interested.

"How'd you hear that?" she asked.

"Waldo over at the saloon told me Skobrak came in there looking for his brother kind'a angry. His brother—David I think is his name—had bought three bottles of whiskey and headed out of town. Had quite a lot of money with him at the time."

Alice digested that while she picked up a bolt of light blue cotton. Now here was some material she could use. It would make a nice dress for Sunday with a little frill on it, and maybe a work dress too.

"I'll take three yards of this," she said, and Cyrus came over and took the cloth.

"So Skobrak is all alone out there with his brother's son?" she asked.

Cyrus took the end of the cloth and measured out three yards, stretching out his arms once, twice, three times. He nicked the edge with a knife and ripped across the material.

"Yup," he said as he put the bolt back and folded the cloth neatly and expertly. He had been a storekeeper a long time.

"Too bad she's tied down with that sick fellow," Alice observed as she took the cloth.

"Yup," Cyrus agreed.

"You know anything about this sick man?" she asked. "Put it on our account, please," she added, waving the cloth. Cyrus nodded and went over to the counter for his book.

"Waldo said he had seen him in the saloon before, maybe two times in the last year. Said he didn't seem like anything special to him," Cyrus said.

"Well, he sure seems special to her," Alice observed.

"Yeah," Cyrus agreed. "Yeah, he does." He paused. "Don't think there is anything romantic there though," he added.

"Me neither," said Alice. She headed for the door.

"Be kind of nice if the two of them were to get together," she tossed back over her shoulder. She didn't have to say which two she was talking about. She didn't see the troubled expression on Cyrus's face.

"Yeah," he said. "It's too bad, but I don't see that happening while that Walter fellow is still holding her back though."

"Me neither." Alice opened the door.

"Be best if that fellow was to get better . . . or die," Cyrus said to her back so quietly she could hardly hear. She turned back to face him.

"Why, Mayor Hanson!" she said. "Not nice to wish a man dead." Cyrus was a little flustered.

"Oh, now that isn't what I meant," he said. "I don't wish anybody dead. I just meant it would be better for those two if he wasn't hanging there around her neck is all."

Alice laughed at his discomfort.

"A sick man can be a burden more ways than one," she said. "Come to think about it, so can a well one," Cyrus heard her laugh as she closed the door behind her. He leaned on the counter and watched her walk away.

"You want to close your eyes a minute, Virginia?" Wiley asked again, voice real quiet.

Virginia had never heard anyone speak so soft and so hard and final at the same time. Time seemed to freeze while she thought that over. David whined softly.

"Don't do it, Virginia," David pleaded. "If'n you close your eyes he will blow my head off for sure." Virginia knew he was right. She had but to close her eyes for an instant and this man was going to have his head shattered right there while he was still on top of her.

The gun didn't move and neither did David. When Wiley finally spoke again, she could sense him struggling to control his anger, could hear the slight trembling in his voice, but his tone was, if anything, even softer than before.

"He is for killing," Wiley said. "Man with no honor don't deserve to live with the rest of us." She heard David moan again, real soft and low in his throat.

"It was the whiskey," he said desperately. "The whiskey made me do this."

"Man's responsible for his actions," came the soft verdict. "Drunk or sober." And that sounded almighty final, both to David and to Virginia.

"Get off'a me," she said to David. "Get off'a me and ride on out of here and remember from now on you are living on somebody else's time."

David looked at her, pleading in his eyes. The gun had not yet budged.

"Go ahead," she said. "He will not shoot you, only get off me and get out of here now." David made up his mind, and slowly rose to his feet, the gun stuck against his ear all the way. He felt his gun pulled from his holster, and then the cool steel barrel was no longer prodding against his ear. He looked at the man holding down on him.

The man was thin, wasted almost, but it was not his physical condition that held David's eyes; it was his expression, the look of contempt, the look of pure, feral hatred. Never had he been closer to death, and likely he never would be again until it was time to cash in and see what was really on the other side. David suddenly wanted to go to relieve himself real bad.

"You owe her your life," said the man, real slow and plain. "I'd keep riding for a long ways if I was you," he added, "on account of if I ever see you again anywhere anytime, I am going to kill you and enjoy doing it."

David swung up on his horse and started him walking away. His head was pounding like it was on fire, but that wasn't the spot of him that felt the worst. He could feel the spot in his back where the man's bullet would hit, could feel it plain as day. That was the spot that felt the worst.

It seemed to take a long time until he felt safe enough to touch spurs and put the horse into a canter, and then he was out of range and could feel the sweat breaking out all over him. He reined to a halt and looked back over his shoulder. The man and woman were gone.

Shame flooded through him. How low a creature he had become! And it was the whiskey that did it, he was sure. He wasn't a bad man, not really. It was the whiskey. It was always the whiskey.

"Darn it!" he said out loud. He fished the bottle out of his saddlebag. Half empty and it was the last one.

Now was the time. He could sink no lower. Now was the time to toss the bottle away, to smash the glass and let that nasty stuff soak into the ground. He would never take another drink, he swore it. He would ride back to town, apologize to Steve, and never, ever let that awful stuff pass his lips again.

He would begin building his life anew; after all, he was a father with a son to set an example for. He smiled grimly. He had set some kind of example for Alfred so far, and that was the truth of it.

David held the bottle up in front of the sun. The tea-colored liquid flopped and rolled inside, washing against the glass as the light sparkled through it. It was hard to believe that something so pretty and innocent-looking could be so hard and controlling on a full-grown man. It didn't look powerful and dangerous. It looked kind of bland and light and sparkly.

He pulled the cork, tilted his head back and let the nectar of life pour down the glass into his mouth.

Chapter Eleven

The two of them stood there side by side and watched David ride away.

"I was going to kill him," Wiley said, slight surprise in his voice.

"I know."

"I wanted to kill him," he went on, almost to himself. "I wanted to blow his miserable head clear off." He looked down at her. "And I would have too, hadn't a been for you."

Virginia suddenly realized her bandanna was lying there at her feet. He could see her head! Her hands flew up to cover her naked scalp and she turned away, bending down to get the bandanna.

"Don't look at me," she said. Her shame burned up her neck and across her face. Her bald head was fire red too, most likely. Her right hand scrabbled in the dirt for the bandanna, her cloth of safety, her barrier against the shame. She felt it there, the soft cloth that had covered her baldness for so many years.

So this was what it was like. She had often thought about it, imagined what it would be like if the unthinkable happened. And now, the worst *had* happened, and two men had seen her most secret disgrace. One of the men she did not care about really. He was a stranger and likely would never pass this way again—at least she hoped not.

The other one though, the other one was Wiley, and she cared what he thought. She cared almighty much what he thought. And now he could see her with her awful naked skull shining in the sun. The big secret was out. It was over.

And then, for some reason, she straightened. The bandanna lay forgotten in the dirt. It was too late for that now. Now all was honesty in the bright light of day. She stood tall as she could, back straight, and turned to face him.

Wiley was still standing there looking down at her, gun hanging loose in his hand. He wasn't looking at her head really, he was looking at her eyes. His expression was unreadable. Virginia stood there motionless and looked back waiting for him to say something . . . anything.

He glanced up at her head for a second, then looked back into her eyes.

"That reminds me," he said. "Potato crop looks pretty good this year," and he turned and walked back toward the cabin.

She felt her chin drop in surprise. She was going to say something, but for a while nothing came out. Nonplussed didn't begin to cover her emotional state.

"What?" she said finally, and then again. "What!"

She stood there absolutely stock-still and watched him walk away while she tried to sort it out in her head. What did he mean by that? How could he make light of her affliction, be so unfeeling, so cruel?

When she heard herself start to laugh it came as an amazing shock. She was laughing! That was coming from her!

She felt the wonderful relief from the constant tension, the relentless fear of discovery. The laughter came bubbling up from somewhere deep inside. She laughed louder, tears welling from her eyes and drawing streaks of mud down her cheeks.

''You bastard!'' she gasped out to him as he walked to the door. It was the first time she had *ever* used the word. ''You miserable bastard!'' and she laughed even harder.

Wiley's face was split wide in a grin as he heard her laughing behind him. For one awful instant there, he had been afraid he said the wrong thing, afraid he had wounded her so badly there could be no forgetting, no forgiving. But she was laughing . . . hard, and the sound was as music to his ears.

He opened the door and went inside, grin splitting his face from side to side. He heard her coming after him, still laughing.

''So you going to pay for another month or what?'' Old Man Tanker asked as he stood there looking down on Marcus in the bed.

''I cannot come up with the money for another month right now,'' Marcus said, trying to sound as pitiful as possible. ''I did not have a lot of money on me when I was shot. I will pay you later if that's all right.''

Tanker never even appeared to hear him.

''Well,'' he said. ''I expect you'll be out by four o'clock, then. That's what time it was when you paid me and that was one month ago today.'' He turned to go, then turned back. ''A contract is a contract,'' he said, and in another minute he was gone.

Marcus looked about for anything handy to throw at the door, to at least symbolically resist the tyrannical old man. But there was nothing, at least nothing he could spare, and he lay back with a sigh. ''A contract is a contract,'' the old man had said, and there was a whole lot of legal truth behind that simple statement. He'd have to be out of there by four or the old man would have the sheriff there by ten after four for sure. He looked out the dirty window to the street outside.

There was nothing for it. He would have to get to his feet, gather his meager stuff together, and go on out on the prairie to live. Likely it would take him another couple of weeks before he could get around without the constant fire coming from his leg where his knee used to be. Funny how something that was destroyed and gone could still hurt so bad. Only it really wasn't funny.

Down the street he saw Walter Waff making his way unsteadily toward the shack. Looked like Walter was half pie-eyed again, likely on Marcus's money too. He was carrying the covered cans that he used to bring Marcus his meals twice a day. It was a job Walter could handle because he didn't have to be stone sober, but the few coins Marcus gave him at a time presented a temptation that sometimes Walter could not resist. So he spent a little on liquor and a little less on food for Marcus.

Sometimes Marcus fumed and fussed to himself something awful about the poor food he was getting, and by now he had sworn to himself that he would just plain disappear Walter as soon as he was well enough to get on without him. But for now he had to swallow his anger and be nice to the only person who was working to keep him alive. Swallowed anger did not make a good stomach companion for poor food.

He was sitting up in the bed when Walter came on in.

"Hi, Walter," he said, actually glad to see the filthy man, even if he *was* drunk. At least he was someone to talk to, someone who came every day.

"'Lo, Marcus," said Walter. His eyes were red, bleary, watering, but he seemed to be as sober as he ever was, which is not to say he wasn't drunk. Marcus idly wondered what it was could make a man waste his life like that.

"Need you to run a couple of errands for me," Marcus said. Walter set the pots on the bedstand.

"Like what?" he wanted to know.

"Need my horse brought over first, then I need you to stop at the store and tell Mayor Hanson to make me up a four-dollar bag of vittles for on the trail. He'll know what to put in it."

"You goin' somewhere?"

"Not for long, friend," Marcus said. Walter considered.

"What's it worth?" he asked.

"Cripes, man," Marcus said. "Don't you have any humanity left in you? Must you get money for every little thing you do for someone else?"

Walter just shrugged. Marcus took stock of his financial situation.

"There's twenty-five cents in it for you," he said finally.

Walter thought on that.

"Fifty," he said flatly. Marcus felt his blood getting hot, but forced himself to stay calm. He was really in no position to bargain.

"All right." He bit off the words. "Fifty cents."

''Deal,'' Walter said. Fifty cents could get him a drink or two at the saloon or a big jar of moonshine from Old Man Tanker. Man could get satisfying drunk on a whole jar of moon. He turned to go.

''Tell Hanson I'll pay him when I pick the stuff up this afternoon,'' Marcus said to his back.

''Sure, sure,'' came the answer, and then Marcus was alone once more and could watch through the dirty window as Walter blundered his way back up the street.

''Fifty cents more,'' Marcus mumbled as he opened the pot and recoiled from the smell of cooked cabbage.

''Damn you,'' he mumbled, then picked up the fork and began to eat.

Mayor Hanson watched Steve ride into town. It was Friday, late in the afternoon. All of a sudden that Skobrak fellow had business in town each and every Friday, it seemed. Sometimes it was to pick up a few supplies at the store. Sometimes it was a stop at the livery. Sometimes Mayor Hanson couldn't tell just exactly *what* Skobrak's business was in town.

But Mayor Hanson—and the rest of the town too—*knew* what the rancher really had in mind when he took off from his day's work and rode into town. His mind was doubtless filled with the nubile form of young Miss Withrow, and that was a fact for sure.

'Course, Skobrak wasn't the only one with a little business in town. Matter of fact, Miss Withrow also had something she was bound to do each and every Friday afternoon just before supper. Seemed only natural that they should accidentally bump into each other every Friday. Of course they would then eat supper together at the café, just a teacher and the guardian of one of her pupils.

It was likely the two of them never suspected that the rest of the town was watching their get-togethers with interest. They probably never guessed that the town was talking about them, about the long silences as they sat together in the café, about the way they looked at each other. Likely the two of them would be embarrassed near to death if they knew they were the topic of such interest and conversation.

But not much happened in a small town. In fact, things had been deadly dull ever since Skobrak had shot that nasty gambler, Marcus Wallers, who had left town two weeks past now.

Before that incident, Skobrak had been in the background, like a man who was there but not worth paying no mind to. But since then he had become noticeably in front of them all. He had stepped forward and saved the virtue of Miss Withrow, and the good women in town looked on him with approval and so did the good men—not that some of the men in town wouldn't like to have a crack at Miss Withrow's virtue themselves.

In any event, the townspeople kept a weather eye on the young couple, and had there been a newspaper, doubtless the two of them would have been mentioned.

All the women thought it was romantic, watching the young couple making the awkward moves of courtship, watching them wanting but not taking. Women seemed to like that kind of prolonged romantic tension, especially married women, likely on account of most of the romance seemed to be gone from their own lives.

The men, on the other hand, liked to imagine

themselves in Skobrak's place, courting this beautiful young woman. Funny how women could never seem to get inside a man's head and understand what he was really about. Men were simple creatures, really. They just needed a little satisfaction to make them practically slaves.

Men and women alike agreed it was a shame that the sick man did not die and leave poor Miss Withrow the opportunity to get a piece of happiness for herself. There seemed to be no question that the nicest thing he could do for her would be to finally pass on to the great beyond and leave the here and now to the well and hearty.

But the man was still lingering with his dying. Old Mrs. Tanker who went inside the cabin on occasion to help out the young woman with her tending the sick, said he was a pathetic shell of a man. ''All skin and bones and not much of a package no more,'' she had said. ''What there is of him is certain full of hurt and suffering.'' She claimed to have never seen a sicker human being in her life, she that had six children die of various diseases at sundry times in her own life.

The mayor watched Skobrak tie up in front of the café and go on inside. Likely he had plumb run out of excuses for being in town. It was no time at all when Miss Withrow came alongside the saloon and crossed the street to the café. Mayor Hanson smiled at his reflection. A pretty girl and a good man. They only needed a little time. He turned back to his figuring.

Supper was over and so was dessert. Now Steve was one dollar and seventy-five cents broker, but he didn't care about the money. He didn't care about anything, except that he had been able to spend another wonderful Friday supper with that beautiful young girl who seemed to spend an awful lot of time in his mind.

They walked out the front door together, walked over to where Lopez was standing tied to the rail.

"Well," Steve said reluctantly. "I guess I should be getting back."

"Yes," said the wondrous beautiful creature of his dreams. "I should be getting back too. Mr. Donnahue probably is wondering what is keeping me."

Steve's eyes clouded at the thought of another man waiting impatiently for this woman, but he said nothing. The way she lived her life was up to her, and there was really something almost noble about her attitude toward this man who had saved her life.

But he didn't want her to go away from him and back to another man. He wanted her to reach up to him and let him pull her to him and hold her close. He wanted to bend down to her and touch her lips with his own real gentle and easy, wanted to feel her warm breath on his cheek and her female softness all the way up and down his body. That's what he wanted. And he wanted it so bad he could hardly stand the wanting anymore.

They were in the shadow of his horse, old Lopez blocking out the lantern light from the café, and nobody could see them or was likely looking anyway. She reached her hand out to him. Steve reached forward and took her small hand in his own.

"Good night, Steve," she said.

Her hand felt so different from a man's hand. It was so small first of all, so slim and soft, and her grip was easy and warm, so skin-to-skin that he felt it jolt all the way up his arm. It almost made him gasp.

" 'Night, Katherine," he said back, but he did

not let go. He would stand there like that all night if she'd let him.

It was amazing to him that something could feel so . . . *lovely* was the only word that fit, even if it was not a word he had used much before in his hard life. That this soft, tapered hand had a real woman attached just seemed so wonderful. And the fact that she was letting him touch her, letting him feel her warmth and soft, was even more amazing. She gently pulled her hand away.

Somehow, Steve found himself aboard Lopez, watching her graceful walk as she went back alongside the saloon and then disappeared into the dark. In a second he heard the closing of her door, heard it clear as anything. He reined Lopez to a walk, then a canter and headed out of town. Every now and then he would smell his hand where he had held hers. He could smell just a tiny taint of her female smell, an aura so faint, so barely not there at all, that it might have been his imagination, only it was not.

Steve and Katie would have been astonished to know that many townspeople had been witness to their brief moment of handholding. They would have been embarrassed to know that they would be the main topic of conversation for the entire town most of the week. All told, six townspeople had been watching—and an awful-looking man with a scraggly growth of beard who had stood in the dark and watched the whole thing.

He watched them hold hands and look at each other, and he watched them part and go their separate ways, Katie to her house and sick man, Steve to ride slowly out of town and back to his ranch and nephew. Then the watcher turned and went back to his horse. He walked with an awful, exaggerated limp that conveyed some of the pain he was suffering and told of the miserable hurt of not having a knee anymore. As he rode out of town in the opposite direction from Steve, the lanternlight from the café shone off his strapped-down gun.

The potatoes were in. It had gone lots faster with two of them working, although at first Wiley could not do much without having to lie down and sleep for hours. Even in the beginning, though, he had helped. Light as he was, he could still put the shovel into the ground with a single step, and weak as he was, he could still turn up the potatoes better than she could.

Virginia sat in front of the fire and sewed a shirt for him while thinking about the large pile of potatoes in the cellar. She also had the rows of canned corn and peas and beans she had harvested that were lined up in the pantry, and knew there was more than enough to keep the two of them through the winter, especially if Wiley could manage to hunt some meat.

The thought of him hunting disturbed her some, for it brought to the front of her mind the one thing she had tried to keep away—his being able to travel.

No doubt about it, the man was getting better fast, and she would occasionally see him looking over the horizon; she knew he was thinking about the man who had shot him. No doubt he would want to go after that man; he had told her so in plain language sure enough. The big question, the one she didn't want to think about, was what he would do after he found the man. Somehow, she didn't know how she could stand being out here all alone again.

Life was so different, so much better having him here. There was someone to talk to once in a while, someone to care about and worry over. There was someone who knew all about her, and still seemed to like her fine. It wouldn't be fair for life to tempt her like that, to show her how fine living could be, and then snatch it away. Surely life wasn't meant to be that cruel, hard, and tormenting. But she knew it was. Life really was hard and mean and only for the tough and unfeeling. Maybe showing her how good it could be and then taking the good away was just a way for life to make her tougher and more self-reliant. But it would be a godawful nasty lesson, and that was for certain.

She looked over at Wiley, asleep in his bed on the floor. Poor thing. He was flat wore out from working all day in the sun, first full day he had been able to manage. She watched the gentle rise and fall of his chest, looked at his face now soft and almost tender in his sleep.

The awful want came inside her, the desire for him to stay and never go away, the desire for him to love her and want to be around her as much as she wanted to be around him. But it was likely not to be, and she had better realize that and adjust to it.

Even though Wiley didn't seem to notice her affliction and never even made any comments or jokes about it anymore, she wondered what man would want a woman who was as ugly and deformed as she was. What man would want a woman he would be ashamed to take to town and show to his friends?

She sighed and looked down on the sleeping man. It was not going to happen. She had better just enjoy the best life could give her while it was still happening, enjoy it now and let the awful aloneness of tomorrow take care of itself. Likely it would be along soon enough. She turned back to her sewing and tried to keep her stitches tiny and even. It should be a good shirt for him, something he would wear until the cloth was thin and no longer kept him warm and covered. At least that much she could give him, that much and likely no more.

Chapter Twelve

The cricket was somewhere just right over there, not more than two or three feet away, but Wiley couldn't see the little fellow. Or maybe it was a girl cricket, for all he knew. The insect was squeaking away in steady chirps, regular and almost monotonous—unless you were another cricket, he supposed.

Overhead the stars burned hard and clear on account of the earlier rain, and everything smelled like early fall, what with the smell of freshly turned dirt and dead leaves from the trees at the creek. The wind blew soft and easy, cool on the cheek, and for the moment, all was right with the world.

Inside he could hear Virginia humming to herself as she finished up the dishes. Sometimes it was good, real good, just to be alive, especially since he so nearly wasn't.

And then Virginia was finished inside and the door opened; he could see her image golden in the lanternlight as she came outside. Then she closed the door and it was dark again and she was standing right there beside him.

The silhouette of her head tilted back as she followed his gaze up into the heavens, and she held that pose for quite a while, drinking in the beauty of the stars on this clear night. Wiley couldn't see her face really, but he could easily see her shape, the shape of her smooth throat, the shape of her cute little upturned nose as she looked up at the stars.

The silence dragged out, but it was not an uncomfortable silence, rather the silence of two people who knew each other pretty well or at least thought they did. Truth be told, they didn't know each other at all.

"Pretty night," Wiley said softly.

"It is," she agreed.

"I am sorry to have been such a bother to you," he said.

Virginia looked over at him and he could see the shape of her ears. She had such pretty ears, he thought. Now there was something you didn't hear a man say too often about a woman. 'Course, the way he felt about her, he pretty much figured she had a pretty everything. Her eyes glinted dark in the starlight.

"You have been a big help to me," she said. "I would not have been near done with the harvest, yet."

"I was not much of a help for the last two months," he replied. "Seems like you paid a mighty high price for a little harvest help."

Somewhere back by the muttering brook, an owl hooted.

"I am not complaining, Wiley," she said after a minute.

"You are not the complaining type," he stated. A breeze rustled the leaves still hanging in the trees, and he could actually hear some of those leaves make that quiet little sound they make as they fell against other leaves already down.

"I am trying to say thank you, I guess," he said, wishing he could see her face. He liked to look at her face, liked to look into her eyes. She was a comfort for a man just to look at. He looked at her a lot, mostly when she didn't know he was looking at her.

Virginia strained her eyes trying to see the face of this man who made her so wondrous and miserable all at the same time. Sometimes she could get a clue as to what he was thinking if she could only see his face, his speckled gray eyes.

"No need to thank me," she said. "You'd have done the same had you found me shot out there and that's the truth of it."

She wondered what it would feel like if he was to hug her—no, more than a brief little hug—if he was to hold her nice and easy, front to front, like she wanted him to. If only he would put his arms around her and hold her soft and gentle. She knew it would make her feel safe and warm for the first time since . . . for the first time ever, she guessed.

The breeze blew easy around her and they stood there inches apart only it might as well have been feet or miles for all that was likely to happen. Even though he made like it wasn't much to him, no man was going to take kindly to a bald-headed woman, and she was pretty sure that was a fact now and would be a fact until the day she died.

Still, it was nice to think on, and couldn't hurt, so she thought about what it would be like to be held by him and the silence stretched out like wrinkled cloth.

"I believe I am well enough to sit a horse," he said, just like he was making casual conversation.

But it cut her so deep, hurt her so much that she caught her breath with the ache of it. No, not yet. Please, not yet. In another week, or another two weeks, she would maybe be ready. Maybe she would be stronger and it would be easier to take. But please, Lord, not yet.

"So you figure you'll be moving on then," she heard herself say. Strangely, her own voice sounded almost normal to her. It should be twisted with fear, with pain, and yet it came out almost normal.

He sighed.

"I reckon," he said and her heart practically stopped, felt like it was broken in two.

"No reason to hurry," she said casually, as if it didn't matter to her one way or another, as if she wasn't all twisted up inside.

The evening dragged on another minute, but there was no longer any beauty about it.

"Might be I could come back and see you now and again," he said. His voice sounded a little strange to her, a little tight, like.

She tried to imagine what it would be like to see him come riding over the hill, riding back for just a friendly visit while she ripped and tore her insides all to pieces. She tried to imagine what it would be like to have to say good-bye again—and maybe again, and again, each time he came by to say howdy. And then would come the time he would tell her about his new woman and she didn't think she could bear that, didn't think she could stand that at all.

She let the silence drag on, and drag it did, as her mind raced frantically, looking for the one thing she could say that would make him stay. But there wasn't one thing. The only one thing she could think of would likely scare him away even faster, maybe even shock him. Maybe it would even make him laugh. And so she said nothing for a long time.

She could feel him waiting for her to say something, waiting for her to invite him back to visit. She could almost feel the surprise in him that she did not. She looked at the silhouette of the man she loved, the man she wanted more than anything else in her whole life.

"Good night, Wiley," she said. She went back inside, and then she was in bed and turned to the wall before she heard the door open as he came in for the last time.

The morning came with the cawing of crows by the creek. And it was crisp outside. Inside, the stoked-up fire made the cabin warm and almost cozy, but the coolness of strained relationships, unfulfilled wants, tainted the air.

Virginia had been up for a long time. She had lain there and looked across the small room at the slow-breathing man asleep on the floor, and then finally she had gotten up. The fall snap in the air brought a glow to her cheeks and woke her for sure on her trip out back. When she came in she was awake and as ready as she could ever be for what the day would inevitably bring.

She placed some wood on the fire and started in to cooking a big breakfast, a man's breakfast, maybe the last one she'd ever have to make. Wiley stirred and opened his eyes as the smell of boiling coffee permeated the room.

"Morning," he said.

"Morning, Wiley," she said, just like it was any other day. He got up, stretched, and went out back. Virginia tended to his bed, rolling the bedroll just like it was when she first found him so many days ago. She had it tied in a bundle and set by the door for him. She put his meager belongings into the saddlebags, and then he was coming back through the door.

Wiley was stunned when he came in and saw his bedroll and saddlebags, standing there waiting for him. It didn't seem possible that just a casual conversation in the beauty of a fall evening would turn into hard reality so soon, yet there was his stuff. Virginia had her back turned, was working on her cooking, and could not see the flash of hurt cross his face. She returned with a cup of coffee, which he took gingerly.

"Thanks," he said.

"Welcome." And she turned back to the fire.

Wiley watched her fussing around fixing his breakfast. She had done so much for him, saving his miserable life, and yet that was not enough as far as he was concerned. He wanted more from her, more than she seemed prepared to give, and it would likely be best for her if he was to leave as promptly as possible. It was clear she was inviting him to be gone, and he owed her so much it wouldn't be right to stay.

But he had enjoyed the last few weeks since he could get around. It had been so nice to hear her humming to herself as she did her chores, so nice to watch her walk to and from the creek, to see the way she moved like a healthy young animal. It had been so nice to talk to her, so easy and unstrained, and she had never really let on that she wanted him gone so bad.

But she had let it on now, and his things stood waiting for him by the door, almost accusing him of overstaying his welcome.

She set the breakfast on the table. It was a lot of food, and suddenly he realized he wasn't very hungry. But he would eat so as not to hurt her feelings, and as he began to fork in the duck eggs and potatoes, he watched her standing by the fire and wished this was just another day like the ones before.

"Nice cool day for riding," she said.

He nodded. She couldn't make it much clearer than that.

"Yup," was the only thing he could think of to say, out loud anyway. And in a while, a long silent while, he was done eating and finished his coffee. Then he pushed back from the table. He took the jacket down from the peg, the jacket that used to belong to her father, the one she had been letting him wear in the cool mornings. He shrugged into the cloth coat and then he was outside and going to the small barn.

Ralph was in the corral out back and was a little wild and hard to catch. He wasn't used to the saddle either, and Wiley had to pull the cinch and then wait for Ralph to breathe out so he could snug it down. He had the same trouble with the packhorse, but eventually he managed. He led the horses to the cabin and tied them to the post. The door opened.

Virginia brought out the bedroll and saddlebags and stood there silently watching as he tied them on behind the saddle and suddenly, just like that, he was ready to go.

"I appreciate the loan of the jacket," he said to her. "I'll see to it you get it back." At least that would give him a chance to come back, to see her once more anyway.

Virginia thought about her father's jacket keeping this man warm, and liked that idea.

"No need to return it," she said. For an instant

she thought she saw disappointment, but that didn't seem likely, not after she just gave him the coat.

Wiley stood there, hands hanging loose at his side.

"Doesn't seem right somehow," he said, "me not being able to do anything for you after you saved my life and all."

Virginia looked up at the man she loved more than life itself, the man she was losing now and forever.

"Just don't waste the rest of your life, that's all," she heard herself say.

They stood there for a full ten seconds of silent eye-to-eye looking, and neither could tell what the other was thinking.

Wiley wanted to reach out and take her in his arms and hug her and maybe never let her go, but he didn't think she would like that much. Likely she'd think he was just as nasty as that other fellow had been, and to tell the truth, he wasn't so sure that wasn't the case.

"I'll not forget you, Virginia," he said, and turned away.

"I'll not forget you either, Wiley," she said as she looked up at him. For a moment there, she had the wild feeling that he was going to reach out to her, but of course that hadn't happened. Likely her bandanna put him off.

But she could pretend he had done that, could pretend he had reached out and held her and said something soft and warm into her ear. She could pretend he had gotten back down from his tall horse and gone back inside and she would never be alone again except at the end of her life. She could stand it then because it wouldn't be for too long.

In a way, she would never be as lonely as she

was before, but she would know it better. Things around the place would remind her of him and she would be able to bring out the memories and study them and it might not be so bad. Only before she had not known she was so alone. Now she would have the newfound silence to remind her, to prod her mind into remembering how wondrous it had been to have him around.

He touched the brim of his hat. ''Obliged,'' he said, and then she was looking at his back and he was riding away, this man she loved. She watched him get smaller as he rode toward the hill, then watched him pause at the top, turn the horse, and look back. He raised his hat and waved it to her, and she never even waved back. He turned away and the hill slowly came up his back as he rode away; then he was gone and she felt her eyes flood and everything blur as she turned and went back inside.

She closed the door gently and leaned against it, feeling the wetness of warm tears sliding down her cheeks leaving thin trails of coolness on her face as she cried silently. Her insides hurt with the awfulness of it all, and it seemed to be more than a body could stand. She was alone again, but it seemed so much more alone than before. She would have to go back to the way life was before Wiley.

She felt the hurt inside, the hurt she didn't think would ever go away.

Virginia slid the bandanna from her bald head, crumpled the soft cloth in her hand, and threw it viciously across the cabin.

''C-A-T, cat. R-A-T, rat. B-A-T, bat,'' said Alfred, reading from the primer as they rode along. Steve looked over at his nephew, who was engrossed in the book. Alfred was learning to read just like he turned to anything else he wanted to do. He was dead serious and did not waste a minute of his day on idleness. Their horses clopped up puffs of dust as they followed the road to town.

''I can remember me doing that,'' Steve said, thinking back to a time when he and David were young boys. ''Me 'n Davey made our own slates on account of we couldn't afford the thirty-five cents they cost. Couldn't afford paper, either.''

''Is this where you tell me about how you had to walk ten miles in the snow every day?'' Alfred had a twinkle in his eye.

Steve shook his head in mock distress.

''I fear this generation isn't going to amount to anything,'' he said. ''Life has just been too easy for you young people.''

''That has been one of my main complaints, sure enough,'' Alfred said, grinning. ''Life is just too easy.''

Steve peered ahead. Was that something on the crest of the hill up there?

''So what do you want to do with the rest of your life?'' he asked. ''You going to continue loafing around and watching me work, or what?'' There was definitely something on the hill, something fairly large and uneven. Dead animal, maybe.

Alfred snorted.

''If you call what I been doing loafing, I am for sure getting out of here before you put me to work.'' He followed his uncle's gaze and saw the same thing.

They put spurs to their horses and cut off the road to see what was what.

The two of them reined in and sat there looking down on the dead steer. It had been shot and a small piece of hindquarter had been removed, likely for the one who shot it to eat. That it was theirs was beyond question, for their brand had been cut off and the small piece of branded flesh had been carefully placed atop the dead animal.

''Wasn't there when I came home from school yesterday,'' Alfred said, looking around. He loosed the thong on his gun and his uncle did the same. They took that action almost without any thought. It was automatic. When a man didn't know for sure what was going on it was best to be prepared for anything.

''Wasn't Indians,'' Steve said. ''They'd have taken the whole thing, not just a little chunk like that. His voice was tight with anger. That was a twenty-dollar animal lying there, and twenty dollars was a lot of money to him right now.

They split up slightly, spreading out away from each other just far enough to be safe, then started riding in ever-widening circles around the dead animal. They found nothing, and came together at the dead steer once more.

''Must've shot him from the road, I guess,'' Alfred said.

''Seems likely,'' said Steve. He sighed and swung down.

''Well,'' he said, ''c'mon down. We'll cut him up and anything we cannot sell in town we will take home and eat ourownselves.'' He slid his knife from its sheath and set to work. In a minute, Alfred was beside him, and they began to butcher the animal right there on the ground.

''Man must've known we'd find this,'' Steve said. ''Seems like he wanted us to find it.''

Alfred grunted and continued carving on the animal. They worked in silence for a while.

"Only man *I* know of who has reason to hate you enough to do this is that nasty fellow you shot over at Miss Withrow's place," Alfred finally said.

"Only one I can think of," Steve agreed. It made sense. A crippled man would naturally have reason to hate the man who did it to him. "Guess there's a lesson here," Steve said, arms deep in the carcass. "Man deserves shooting is a man who deserves killing."

They worked on for a while, the silence broken only by the wet, sticky sounds of butchering.

"Man hates you this much ain't likely to quit with cows," Alfred observed.

Steve glanced at the lad for a second.

"You are smarter than I gave you credit for," he observed. "It always surprises me when I catch you thinking like a full-grown man."

Alfred smiled a smile of genuine pleasure. He wanted his uncle to think he was a man. Being a man was important to him.

The loud snapping of a pistol being cocked just over there froze the two of them, arms deep in the beef. They slowly turned their heads only and looked up at the man slouched casually on his horse looking down at them. His position was casual, but the way he held his forty-five told them both that he was not a man to be trifled with. Steve mentally cursed at himself for being taken so easily. It was not like him, not like him at all. He suspected that maybe this man was very good at hunting men, very good indeed.

"You boys think maybe the man who owned that beef might be a little put out that you shot it?" Wiley asked. The two stayed rock still. Good.

"Beef is mine," said Steve. "And we didn't shoot it, neither." He saw the badge on the man's chest and relaxed. He stayed motionless while the lawman sorted things out. The man looked a little piqued to Steve.

"What's your name?" Wiley wanted to know.

"Name's Steve Skobrak," said the man. "This here is my nephew, Alfred."

Wiley noticed the primer tucked into the young boy's saddle.

"You own a Sharps rifle?" Wiley asked casually.

"Nope," Steve replied. He nodded at the rifle protruding from the boot under his saddle. "Winchester's the only long gun I own. Boy has one too." It was really his brother's gun, but since Davey was gone it only seemed right that Alfred should have it.

"What you planning on doing with the meat?" Wiley asked.

"Going to sell it in town, least what I can," Steve said. He didn't like being under another man's gun, but he held still and quiet just the same. "We'll take the rest back to the ranch for ourownselves," he added.

"That the place just up the road?" Wiley asked.

"Yup."

Wiley looked the man in the eye and made up his mind. He let the hammer down and holstered his gun but did not put the thong on the hammer.

"Tell you what," he said. "You boys can finish butchering that thing and we'll just ride on into town together." He waited for the reaction. Steve shrugged.

"That'll be just fine, Marshal," he said. "Matter of fact, I kind'a like seeing the law looking out for my beef the way you are." He turned back to his butchering.

Alfred looked steadily at the lawman, who gazed back impassively.

"You look kind'a tired, Marshal," Alfred observed.

"Been a long day, son," Wiley said.

Alfred studied the man for another second. Seemed like there was more to it than just tired. The man looked washed out. Was he sick? Alfred turned back to the butchering with his uncle.

Wasn't half an hour and they were all mounted and riding toward town. The lawman hung back slightly, doing it real casual-like, but never letting either of the two behind him. He hadn't taken their guns, and that had impressed Steve some because it meant the man was good enough that he figured the two of them were no threat. 'Course, their guns were thonged down and his wasn't.

"Seems kind of young to be packing a gun," Wiley observed of Alfred.

"Never figured that age was what it took to make a man a man," Steve said in response. For some reason, Wiley liked that answer. So did Alfred.

"He know how to use it?" Wiley asked.

"I taught him," said Steve.

"That doesn't answer my question," Wiley observed.

"Knows how and knows when too," Steve said bluntly.

"Good thing for a man to know," Wiley affirmed.

Alfred heard himself called a man, heard it from his uncle, and that man's opinion meant more to him than anyone else's in the world. He heard the lawman call him a man too, and that just about made it official far as he was concerned.

He began to understand. It was actions, not age.

He was proud to be called a man, and he could feel the desire to let himself get swollen with pride. Only it wasn't the kind of thing a man would do. It was the kind of thing a boy would do.

He vowed not to let his uncle down. He was a man now, and he would do the rest of his life as a full-grown man and never be a boy again. Somehow he knew that would be a lot tougher than it sounded.

He could feel the stickiness from the butchering drying on his hands and arms. It would be good to wash up.

In twenty minutes the town appeared over the hill and the three men rode down onto Front Street, the marshal trailing slightly.

Chapter Thirteen

Walter wanted to twist and turn, wanted to squirm away from the ceaseless godawful pain gnawing at his insides, but he was too exhausted. The pain was worse than ever, as if something alive was eating him inside out, chewing off bites of his belly, tearing and ripping at his innards, then setting the gaping wounds afire.

He could feel death coming. Life was going to be over, and he didn't even care really. Almost anything would be better than the relentless agony he had suffered. Months of awfulness wore on a man, and he was tired, ever so tired. Now the fighting and struggling was about over.

He knew he was dying, knew it with a certainty that separated him from the world of the living and would have brought a calmness to him if only he didn't hurt so bad all over. Sometimes, over there in the dim corner of the room, he could see the wavering forms of the men he killed. They were waiting patiently, unhurried. Likely they enjoyed watching him suffer so. And they scared him worse than any thought of death.

Those men owed him plenty, and somehow he

knew that once he had passed from the company of living men, his real agony, their godless vengeance, would begin. They would take retribution for the years of life he had snatched away, and they were just waiting there, dim and wavering, dripping and drooling their own gore, the gore he had blasted from their living bodies. They were waiting for the man who killed them.

Someone moved close to him and he forced his eyes to focus back on the real world. It was Katie, beloved Katie. Her father was one of the specters waiting for him, but she could not see him of course.

"Is it bad, Walter?" she asked.

"Oh, God, yes," he said, voice so weak he could hardly hear it himself. He wanted to tell her that the pain was unbearable, that he was afire inside. He wanted to tell her that even though the pain was intolerable, the disappointment was even worse, and so was the fear.

Only yesterday he had been getting better, and hope had begun to grow like a seed in his brain. Then, just like so many times before, he woke in the middle of the night with his hands and feet afire and his insides tearing themselves to shreds. He woke screaming, and was surprised when he recognized the awful keening voice as his own.

"More laudanum," he said.

"I can't, Walter," she said back. "You have had it all." She held the empty bottle for him to see.

"Please," he pleaded. "Get me more. I cannot stand the pain any longer."

"I do not want to leave you," she said, and he thought about that. He would likely die alone if she went out for more, and he did not want to die alone. It seemed so unfair that he was dying now. Only yesterday he had been getting better, had even begun to eat once more.

And that was the worst of this illness, the cycles of hope and crushing disappointment. Soon, these would be over too, and were it not for those wavering forms patiently waiting for him, Walter thought that it would be a good thing.

He decided he would not ask her to get more laudanum. A man could stand the pain on account of he couldn't really get away from it. He *had* to take it. But the horrible, crushing disappointments after the healings were almost worse than the pain itself.

He would start to get better; he would begin to draw away from the pain and awful twisting inside, would even begin to feel hungry and a little stronger. Then, with crushing certainty, the pain would return, always just a little worse than the time before.

He closed his eyes and felt Katie's cool hand resting on his forehead. How he loved that woman. That she could so selflessly devote herself to him in his time of need still amazed him.

Doubtless she would mourn his passing. She would probably wear black and weep and decry his passage for maybe a year or more. In a way, the thought appealed to him. Likely she would be the *only* one to feel bad about his death. On the other hand, there was her father, wavering over there in the corner. Leaving his daughter mourning for her father's killer would likely add untold suffering to his life in the beyond.

If he told her, she would revile him. He could almost imagine the horror and revulsion that would slide over her face when she realized the awful thing he had done. It would hurt him to see her repulsed by him, but he was not going to be with her much longer, and was likely going to be with her father for eternity.

A fresh spear of pain sliced slowly through his bowels, tearing an involuntary gasp from his lips, and now a new section of his insides was on fire. He opened his eyes and looked up at the woman he loved. The time for confession was upon him, and the feeling of impending loss, the loss of her respect, only added to his suffering.

In spite of the exhaustion, the pain, the godawful misery, he decided to tell her. Death was very near, he could accept that now. Death, a blessed relief from the endless weeks of suffering, the long dragging seconds and minutes and hours of teeth-clenched agony.

"K-K-Katie," he said weakly. "Your father. I must talk to you about your father."

"What, Walter?"

He took a deep breath that hurt something awful.

"I am the one what killed him," he said simply. He did not have enough energy left for emotional speeches or explanations.

Katie waved one hand as if trying to push the impossible information away.

"Oh, Walter," she said. "You always did think I was such a foolish young girl."

It was the reaction Walter had expected, feared almost. She obviously didn't believe him, didn't believe him now when it was so vitally important that he be believed. The wavering form of her father swam into view for a moment, but it was not the specter that drove him.

Now, when it was too late, he finally loved something, someone. For the first time in his miserable life he wanted to give rather than take, diminish suffering rather than spawn it, ease a mind instead of inducing even more torment. She hovered over him in his hour of dying, a soft-faced lovely young woman. And he loved her—selflessly.

In spite of the pain, the exhaustion, the godawful misery, he tried again.

"I killed him," he said.

Katie looked down on him, eyes full of something. What was it? Compassion? Then her expression changed, quick as you could slam a window. It was a new expression, something he had never seen before and it took a moment for him to identify it as what it was.

"I know you killed him, Walter," she said, voice suddenly very cold, emotionless almost. "I've known it all along. That's why . . . ever since that very first night out on the prairie . . . I've been poisoning you."

Walter's eyes opened wide. Was she fooling him? Trying to make a joke? He looked into her eyes, her deadly serious eyes.

"Arsenic, Walter," she said blandly. "In your coffee." She smiled. "You did complain about my coffee a lot," she added.

And then he knew.

All those months of suffering, all the pain and agony, all the spewing of stuff from his body, all that was retribution for what he had done. This young woman had avenged the wrong he did her, avenged it a hundred times over, a thousand times over. He felt the fire twist in his belly.

"I hate you, Walter," she said, hard and clear. "You can't imagine how much I hate you." She was beginning to warm to her task, to take some pleasure in finally being able to tell him what she had wanted to say so many times before.

"I look at you and get the same feeling I get when I see a snake slithering in the dirt. You make my skin crawl. You make my stomach twist up inside me." The hatred was plain in her voice. Walter lay there and looked up at this face he once thought was angelic.

Inside his belly a fire raged, seared, ate his being slowly and gleefully. He knew now, knew it was a fire set by her. He felt the deadness of his feet and lower legs. It was as if they were no longer there, except he had a sensation of weight where they were supposed to be. It was death, creeping up his body slowly, consuming him for the one final time, sending him to the other world, the one with the godawful specters. Looking up at the woman he loved, he thought that maybe facing the specters would be easier now.

"Father was a teacher, Walter," she said in a suddenly conversational tone. "I'm sure I told you that before. His favorite subject was chemistry. I learned quite a lot from him actually." She looked down on him as one might look at a frog on a rock.

"Hurts, doesn't it," she said and smiled her angelic little smile. He lay there and wondered at how he could have been so wrong, so deceived.

"I hate you for killing Father," she said in the same bland tone, "but I hate you even more for what you made of me." She shook her head in amazement.

"I never could have imagined myself doing violence to another living being," she said. "Now look at me, killing you slowly and in the most painful way possible. And enjoying it, loving it, even." She rested her hand gently on his forehead.

"That pain you feel, Walter," she said. "I gave

you that.'' She smiled, looking like nothing more than a pleased child.

''I gloried in your suffering,'' she went on. ''I enjoyed letting you get almost better, then slamming you down again and again.'' She took her hand away and stood there beside him. ''You killed my father you . . . you . . . awful, evil man.'' The deadness was past his hips now, and the awful bright pain in his belly seemed to be moving away, growing more and more distant.

''I am not a particularly religious person anymore,'' she said. ''You killed that too. But in case I am wrong, in case there is a God, there is something I want to say, some words that have never passed my lips before. I want them to be the last words you will ever hear.'' She bent her face down close to his, looked him deep in the eyes.

''God damn you, Walter,'' she hissed.

For an instant his astonishment overcame even the pain, and as the heavy deadness finally overtook him, that was his expression as he died.

Katie reached over and gently closed his wide eyes. She sighed and looked down on him.

It was finally over.

It was time, as far as Marcus was concerned.

True enough, his leg was not all the way healed, but he had been living out on the godforsaken prairie long enough . . . too long.

There had been some satisfaction in killing that cowboy's beef last night, but it was not enough, would never be enough even if he killed every one of the stupid, smelly animals. It had to be the man himself, and it had to be slow and hurtful. Plenty hurtful. But not too slow.

And so he rode back into town, keeping out of

sight. He had no real plan, no sure idea how to kill the man without risking death or jail, but he did know where to find the man, sure enough. It was just a matter of time. All he had to do was watch the woman.

He scratched at his scraggly beard and tried to brush some of the prairie dust from his clothes as he lounged around, out of sight just inside the door of the small livery barn across the street from the saloon. It was a good spot. He could easily see anything that happened in the alley she traveled, yet would not likely be seen by her or anyone else.

It looked like it was going to be his lucky day, because he had barely got himself settled down on some hay, stiff leg stuck out in front, when his quarry came riding into town. He was with a boy and another man, but Marcus could wait. He would actually enjoy the waiting. It was quite a rush watching his mortal enemy and knowing he was soon to be writhing in agony on the ground—and the woman too.

''Yup,'' said Sheriff Foy. ''That's his ranch, sure enough.''

Wiley relaxed in the saddle, allowing the deep weariness to flow over him.

''Figured it was, the way he was acting,'' he said to Foy. He turned to Steve. ''Sorry about that.''

''No harm done,'' said Steve. ''Glad to see you protecting my beeves.'' He reined his horse and turned away, beef to sell.

Wiley nodded and turned back to Sheriff Foy. ''Reason I am in town in the first place is on account of I am looking for a man and a woman who came through town in a wagon maybe three, three and a half months ago.'' It was not lost on him when Steve suddenly reined his horse to a stop. ''Man likely has a Sharps rifle,'' Wiley added.

''What did they do?'' The sheriff looked pained, and Wiley had a sudden hunch.

''They're still here, aren't they?'' he asked.

''Sheriff!'' It was a woman calling from across the street. She hurried over. Wiley sensed the tenseness in Steve; he could feel the electricity in the air and wondered what was going on. It was like Steve was suddenly dangerous, and the sheriff was tense. Wiley didn't like the situation at all. Now, what could have brought all this on?

''Sheriff, I am glad you are here,'' said the woman as she came up to them. Wiley saw the way Steve glanced at her from atop his horse and suddenly understood. This was the woman, and Steve had more than a passing interest in her.

''What's the problem, Miss Katie?'' asked the sheriff.

''He is dead,'' she said, weariness in her voice. ''He got worse again this morning and suffered something fierce all day and just died right now.'' She looked up at Wiley with slight curiosity, then looked back at the sheriff.

Foy sighed. He wasn't quite sure how to handle all this.

''I am sorry, Miss Katie,'' he said. ''Seems a shame, what with all your hard work caring for him and all, but it maybe is for the best.''

''For the best?'' she asked. She glanced over at Steve, who was watching intently. She smiled a little sad smile and he nodded back and touched his hat . . . with his left hand. His right was still resting loose on the saddle horn. Not too far from his gun.

''He was suffering something awful,'' said Foy. ''Sometimes death can be a blessing, you know.''

''This is her, isn't it?'' Wiley asked. There was an expectant pause, then Foy nodded, almost unwilling to let on. Katie's head turned to Wiley.

''What do you mean, 'this is her'?'' she asked.

Wiley removed his hat with his right hand, careful to move slow, watching Steve from the corner of his eye.

''Sorry, Miss,'' he said. ''My name is Wiley Board, Marshal Wiley Board, and I have been looking to meet you for over three months. Tell the truth, I figured you were dead.''

''I don't understand,'' she said calmly.

''That man with you,'' Wiley came back. ''He own a Sharps rifle?''

''Mr. Donnahue had a rifle yes,'' she said. ''I'm afraid I don't know one kind from the other.'' She realized for the first time something strange was going on. She looked from Wiley to Steve to the sheriff. ''What's going on?'' she asked.

''I believe that man, Mr. Donnahue, is the one who killed a man in your wagon and tried to murder me,'' said Wiley. He didn't feel so tired anymore.

''I'm afraid you are mistaken,'' she said. ''Mr. Donnahue is the one who saved me from the Indians. He came to my aid and helped me get safely away from them.''

Wiley studied her for a moment.

''I see,'' he finally said. ''I'd like to meet him anyway, Miss,'' he said. ''Maybe he can explain how I got so mixed up.''

Her face twisted in . . . grief?

''I am sorry,'' she said, ''but it seems you are a day too late. Mr. Donnahue just passed away.'' She looked down. ''It was not a pleasant passing, either,'' she mumbled.

Steve swung down and walked over to her. He had his hat in his hand.

"I am sorry, Katie," he said, real soft. "I know you did all you could." Suddenly Katie was crying and it seemed natural that they should be holding each other. Wiley noticed the surprised expression on the boy's face as he looked down at them, and almost smiled.

"She's the town's teacher," Foy said. "Been doing a good job too."

Now Wiley understood the surprise on the lad's face. The boy was still going to school, and teachers were never human beings, not to their students. The idea that a teacher could cry and feel bad, or, wonder of all wonders, hug a man, would be real shocking to anyone who only saw her in the classroom. Some folks felt the same about lawmen.

"Might be," said Wiley to Foy, "that we could take a look at this man's rifle."

"Surest thing," said Foy. He turned aside to the boy. "Alfred," he said. "Best be you go get Wentworth and tell him he has a burying to prepare for. He can come and get the body soon as can be."

"Yes, sir." The boy touched his hat and was gone down the street.

"Follow me," said Foy, and he led off across the street. Wiley reined his horse to walk after him. Steve mounted up and did the same. Wiley noted the slight shock on the woman's face and wanted to smile, but didn't. She was surprised at Steve getting on his horse and leaving her to walk like that. Apparently she didn't know about cowhands, didn't know they would never ever walk when they could ride. Steve likely didn't even think about it, but just swung aboard.

And so the four of them went down the alley and

inside. It was obvious Katie was not too anxious to go back in there, but Steve stayed right with her.

Walter was lying there in bed, dead. He had a weird expression on his face for a dead man, but who knew what he was thinking when he died.

"First time I seen him look anything like peaceable since he got here," Foy observed. "He did some almighty suffering before he passed on, and that's a fact." Wiley looked down on the man. So that's what he looked like, the man who shot him . . . maybe.

"You never heard nobody complain about their hands and feet like he did," Foy went on. "Kept hollerin' they was on fire."

Wiley looked up sharply.

"I heard somebody die like that before," he said flatly. Katie looked steadily across the room at him and he gazed right back.

"Wasn't catching, was it?" Foy wanted to know.

"Nope," said Wiley and favored Katie with a grim smile. "Wasn't catching." Her expression did not change.

"Here's his rifle," said Foy, picking up the weapon from where it leaned against the wall. He handed it over and Wiley studied it. It was a Sharps, 50-caliber, sure enough. There was a shell in the chamber.

He walked over to the door, stuck the rifle outside, and triggered off the round. The thing kicked like fury and the sound trapped between the two buildings was more like a roar than a bang. He ejected the shell and caught it in his hand.

The casing was hot, and he flipped it from hand to hand until it was cool enough to study. It matched the one in his saddlebags, sure enough. He had found the killer and the man who tried to kill him.

Wiley walked over to the bed and looked down on the evil man.

"He died hard, huh?" he asked.

"Suffered something fierce," Foy agreed.

Katie watched Wiley from where she was standing next to Steve.

"Well," said Wiley. "This is the man who killed the man in the wagon and tried to kill me, sure enough."

"You mean he killed her paw and then wormed his way into her good graces?" Foy asked, surprise evident in his voice.

"That's a fact," Wiley said flatly. Foy turned to Katie.

"I guess you don't have to mourn him none," he said. Katie said nothing, watching Wiley like a cornered bird might watch a snake.

"Hands and feet on fire, huh?" Wiley said, almost to himself.

"Yup," Foy said. "Not a good way to die." He paused. "Guess the Lord sometimes takes care of business real good," he added.

Wiley smiled a tight little smile at Foy. "Yup," he said. "Guess he does, sure enough."

Wiley turned to go, taking the Sharps with him. He opened the door and stepped through, then turned back. Wiley looked at Katie, studying her, face serious. His badge shone polished on the front of his vest. She waited, almost holding her breath. Wiley looked at Steve.

"Be in your best interest to take real good care of that woman," he said.

"Figured on it," was the laconic reply.

Wiley grinned broadly at Katie, tipped his hat. "Miss," he said. And then the door was closed and they could hear him get on his horse and clip-clop up the alley.

"What did he mean by that, I wonder," Steve asked.

Katie looked up at the man she loved.

"I have no idea," she said.

Marcus had found that rubbing his leg sometimes made the nagging residual pain diminish some, and already it had developed into a habit. He hardly knew he was doing it anymore, and he sat there and rubbed on his leg while he waited for the perfect opportunity to get that cowboy and the woman alone, preferably together. He was prepared to wait as long as it took, likely days and maybe weeks. The time would be spent imagining the upcoming revenge, and sometimes imagining their brutalization was almost as satisfying as the real thing was going to be.

As he watched the comings and goings in the alley over there, he figured that it was likely the sick man had finally died. He found he didn't care about that one way or the other. The extra lawman who showed up bothered him some, but after a while the lawman had come out of the alley and ridden down the street toward the edge of town. With any luck he would keep on going.

Hardly any time at all passed before the cowboy and the woman came out of the alley leading his horse. It didn't seem possible that his plans were going to work out so soon, but it looked like they were coming across to the livery barn.

In a way, Marcus was slightly disappointed. He had been looking forward to resting in the hay and imagining awful ways to get even, awful things he could do to the two of them. Now it looked like he wasn't going to be given a whole lot of time to enjoy planning, because sure enough, they came into the barn.

They didn't see him at first, sitting there with his gun in his hand, and he made no sound, preferring for them to discover him in their own time.

"I am glad you are going to stay in town tonight," she said as they walked in.

"Me too," said the cowboy. And then the cowboy looked into the depths of the small barn and saw the man sitting there holding a gun on them. The cowboy froze and the woman gasped as she followed his gaze and saw the gun.

Steve recognized the man. Darn! He had broken one of his own rules and now he stood likely to pay the piper. If you find it necessary to shoot someone, you should make sure he's dead. He knew that. He slowly pushed the woman so she was behind him.

"Howdy," Marcus said.

"Howdy," Steve returned.

It was like the world outside the open barn doors had ceased to exist. All that mattered was happening inside, closed in by four slatted wooden walls. Steve's horse stomped on the ground nervously but Steve and Katie didn't move.

"You made a cripple out'a me," Marcus said.

"Better'n a corpse," Steve observed. He could feel Katie's hand sliding around his waist real slow and easy, following his gunbelt toward his holster.

"Not much," said Marcus. " 'Course, you'll know if that's true in just a minute or so."

"Gonna kill me, huh?" Steve asked, calm and easy.

"Not in any hurry," Marcus said. "Since I'm gonna be a cripple the rest of my life, I'd kind'a like to make this last awhile." He casually waved the gun around, but never got careless. Steve could feel her hand touching the gun butt, shifted slightly to the right to conceal her actions better.

"No need to make the woman watch," Steve said. Keep the man talking. Keep him talking long as possible.

"She'd been a little friendlier, none of this would have happened," Marcus observed. "Seems like you'd want her to be a part of the finish."

"Nope," Steve said.

"Too bad, on account of I figure on doing her too . . . first, maybe." Marcus kept his voice calm and cool, but Steve felt a shiver go up his back. No doubt the man meant every word. Katie tried to lift his gun, but the hammer thong kept it down. Her fingers slid to the front of the holster to unhook the cursed little leather thong. Steve raised his hands in the air, trying to keep the killer's attention away from what was happening at his waist.

"You want I should put my hands up here?" he asked.

"Does not matter," Marcus assured him, toying with him like a cat with a mouse. He was enjoying this plenty.

"I figure on starting at your ankles," Marcus said. "Figure on shooting both of them. Then the knees, and the hips and any other place I can think of where you won't die right away."

Steve felt beads of sweat form on his forehead.

"Where you figure the rest of the town is going to be while you're doing all this shooting?" he asked. Marcus appeared to think on that. Steve felt the thong come loose, felt her hand slide back to the butt of his gun.

"Good point," Marcus said. "Guess maybe I'll

just have to shoot and run.'' He gave a nasty laugh. ''I mean shoot and hobble,'' he said, voice bitter.

He pulled back the hammer on his gun, voice suddenly hard.

''Ma'am,'' he sid. ''I'd sure appreciate it if you'd turn loose o' that gun and step out here where I can see you better.''

Steve felt Katie hesitate, then release her grip on his gun and move out beside him. He made up his mind to go for his gun first chance, slightest chance. There was nothing to lose really, since this man meant to kill them both for certain.

''You ever want to see what the insides of your ankles looks like?'' Marcus asked. Steve felt chilled by the emotionless tone of the man's voice. Marcus did not give him a chance, no opening, and Steven tensed himself to take the shock of a bullet, tensed himself to go for his gun.

''Say good-bye, cowboy,'' said Marcus. The toying was over. The game was done. He aimed down at the man's ankle. First the cowboy . . .

The sound of a forty-five smashed into the quiet barn, and Steve went for his gun and fired almost at the same time. His slug smacked into the chest of the cripple, but his slug was too late, for the man was already falling backward, head snapped back by the heavy slug from Alfred's smoking gun. Katie opened and closed her mouth, but no sound came out as she tried to fight back the shock and horror of what she had just seen and been a part of.

The dead man's hand twitched reflexively when he hit the ground, and his gun discharged into the floor, making them all jump again.

Alfred let his hammer down and eased the smoking weapon back into his holster. He had just killed a man, and that would take some getting used to for sure. Childhood was firmly put away in the brief instant it took for him to squeeze the trigger.

He looked at his teacher standing there, obviously shocked almost out of her reason, and saw beyond the teacher to the woman, to the person.

"I believe she could use a hug," he suggested to Steve, who also seemed to be stunned into inaction.

Almost like an automaton, Steve turned and took the stiff woman in his arms. So many times he had imagined holding her, so many times he had wanted to have her warm and soft against him, but now he barely noticed. It just seemed so natural a thing to do, even while his mind was still racing over the past few seconds.

"Glad you showed when you did," he finally said to Alfred, who favored him with a tight little smile.

"I believe you mean that for sure," he said, then turned and headed away. He needed some time alone, some time to try to make room in his life for the thing he had done.

Footsteps pounded across the street as people came to see what all the excitement was about.

Outside of town Wiley reined in to a stop. Gunshots, sure enough. He sat there with his horse half turned toward town, half facing out into the empty prairie . . . the almost empty prairie. There *was* someone out there, sure enough, and he knew right where she was.

But he was a lawman, and as a lawman it was his duty to ride back, to find out who had just died and why. A lawman could not stop being a lawman, not for himself, not for someone else. He was a lawman twenty-four hours a day. The badge weighed heavily on his chest, and his fingers absently came up to touch the cheap metal thing.

He had worked hard for that badge, risked his life, spent countless nights under the stars, in the rain. He had chased bad men and caught some. He had been shot at and mostly missed, made a few friends and quite a few enemies. He had been scared many times, all the way scared down to his middle. He had earned that badge. It was how he made his living.

He toyed with the cheap metal thing, absently feeling the round little nubs at the end of each spoke. He thought about the short little bald-headed woman out there, and he thought about his duties and responsibilities as marshal. He thought about his old friend Nestor, now married and settled down.

Wiley sighed and looked around. If he was going back, he'd better get moving. It was his job.

The pin on the back of the badge gave a quiet little "*ping*" when he pulled it loose. He slid the badge in his pocket, then reined around and touched spurs. He moved off into the prairie, the town growing smaller behind him until the tall grass just swallowed it up.

Next day, a small, bald-headed woman looked up from where she knelt by the creek doing her laundry. It was proving very difficult to get the bedding truly clean, what with the dried bloodstains and all.

For the hundredth time that day her eyes scanned the horizon, looking for any signs of the someone she didn't want to admit she was looking for. For the hundredth time there was nothing, just the small hills and the clouds and the gentle wind.

It was a lovely fall afternoon.

The creek danced and sang at her feet, an unhurried crystal stream that meandered through the cool shade of the trees. Clear water exposed a bottom that supposed it was hidden and submerged rocks pushed bulges against the surface and sucked bubbles from the quiet air. It was music to keep the fish alive, music to keep her soul alive. But these past several days it did not seem to help.

She watched idly as a water drop trembled at the tip of a leaf, clinging to the living green, fighting against the gravity of itself. Finally, bloated full of miniature images, it fell back into the running stream. She almost imagined she could hear the lone lovely note it made as it plopped into the water, but of course the noise of the stream made that impossible.

She sighed and once more began to work lather from the stained sheets, rubbing them with a big yellow bar of lye soap.

The next time she looked up, there he was.